# A Ratchet City Hustler's Unexpected Halloween Surprise

# Table of Contents

# A Ratchet City Hustler's Unexpected Halloween Surprise

## By

## Renessa D. Jackson

# OTHER TITLES BY AUTHOR

Luvin a Young Ratchet City Boss

Luvin a Young Ratchet City Boss 3$^{rd}$ EDITION

# COPYRIGHT

# TABLE OF CONTENTS

# CHAPTER ONE THE DAY THAT CHANGED EVERYTHING

**M**y day kicked off just like any other day. I was up with the sun at 6am, out on these Shreveport streets, hustlin' like I was born to do. We locals call our city Ratchet City and I'm out here grindin' hard every day makin' moves and power plays. I am a businessman and my business is providing these streets with high quality products of the pharmaceutical kind. My position is sergeant and I am responsible for the Waterside, Highland, Shreve Island, and Broadmoor Subdivisions. My Boss is that nigga Stone and he always provides me with that premium cut pure cocaine, marijuana, and prescription drugs. Ain't nobody out here touchin' the quality we got it's the best on the market.

Hustlin' has always come easy to me, it's all I know and life has been good on the hustle front. No beef in the streets and business has been running smooth lately. But my personal life is a whole other matter, and it's what's got me stumped right now.

I ain't had nothing real relationship wise in over five years. That's when the love of my life, Kiara Kelly walked out and left me high and dry. Since then, I have just been keeping things casual with random hook-ups when the need hit. After K left no one has even sparked my interest to make me want anything beyond a couple nights of raw passion. Lettin' someone besides K in never even crossed my mind and no one has touched my heart.

I thought maybe something was different with Constance Bradley, my current situation, and I might be able to open up and let her in. She don't stir any emotional feelings within me, but she knew how to satisfy me sexually. Right now, that's all I require of a woman so she has been serving her purpose well. But something ain't right with her and I can't quite put my finger on what it is. Then she has me here looking stupid as hell posted up at Unique Nail Boutique on Kingston Road. She hit me up two hours ago begging me to come scoop her, talking 'bout *"baby, please"* and all that sappy shit. Now I've been sitting in this fancy ass reclining chair for damn near an hour, getting my feet worked on 'cause she said she'd *"be done shortly."* Yeah, aight. Shortly came and went forty-five minutes ago.

I ain't even gonna front though, the lil' foot massage was a'ight. They handled my dogs with care, for real. It took off all the rough skin on my hills and removed the corns on my toes. But see, I ain't the type of nigga to be camped out in no nail shop all day like I ain't got nothing better to be doin'. Right when I was 'bout to tell the nail tech I'm out is when some words floating over from where Constance was sitting with Breanna Wilson caught my attention and made my blood run cold.

Breanna Wilson. That name alone got my jaw clenching. She's Kiara Kelly's first cousin, and everybody in these streets know she got that viper tongue, especially when she feeling some type of way. Back when I was with Kiara, Breanna was forever trying to slide in my DMs on some sneaky shit, causing all kinds of family drama. Even after me and Kiara split, shawty kept tryna shoot her shot, but I wasn't having none of that snake energy. Her character is flawed as hell and I ain't fucking with no snake, not even in shoes.

Sitting here now, I'm feeling mad exposed. Like every eye in this bitch is watching me, judging me. You can call me paranoid or whatever, but my gut keeps screamin' for me to bounce. These strangers already all up in my business, hearing whatever snake shit Breanna whispering to Constance. I know that hoe ain't missing out on this opportunity to drop mad salt on me.

The nail tech working on my feet probably thinking I'm some kind of lame, letting this hoe play on my top. The old lady under the foot dryer been trying not to stare, but I see her side eyeing me. Even the little girl getting her first pedicure with her mama keeps looking my way. It's a dead give away that I'm them hoe's main topic of conversation.

In my head, I'm running back all the times, Constance has been acting funny lately. Making me wait, coming up with excuses, always running late. Now I'm wondering if this whole thing, making me sit here like some kind of simp, was planned. Got me feeling like a straight clown, like some kind of joke for the whole shop to laugh at.

The more I think about it, the more my blood pressure is rising. Constance knows exactly what she's doing, having me wait while she kicked it with snake ass Breanna of all people. This that disrespect I been sensing but ain't want to believe. And Breanna? She probably loving every second of this, seeing me uncomfortable, knowing she about to stir up some more drama. That's her whole M.O., can't nobody in the hood trust her fake ass.

But the words I just caught floating over got me frozen to my seat though. And the way Breanna keeps looking over here now, whispering and giggling? Yeah, this whole scene about to be some whole other type of situation. 'Cause these hoes got me all the way fucked up.

*"Constance, girl, have you heard?"* Breanna's voice dripped with that fake sweet talk. The poison she's known for spreadin'. *"Kiara been struggling, all 'cause she's raising Treylon's child alone. I don't know how she kept that secret this long."*

Them words hit me hard, square in my solar plexus. My whole body went rigid, hands gripping the armrests so tight my knuckles went white. K had my child? Nah, this can't be right. I leaned forward, ears straining to catch every word, praying I heard wrong.

*"What you mean, Bre?"* Constance's voice wavered, but that undertone, something about it ain't sit right with me.

*"Girl, Treylon got Kiara pregnant five years ago. She ain't tell him 'cause he was always talking 'bout he ain't want no kids. So, she left. Now she out here grinding hard working two jobs, barely keeping her head above water to raise their son. Ain't that some shit?"* Breanna's laugh was ugly, full of that jealous energy she carried.

*"Why you bringing this up now? You know he's just across the way,"* Constance hissed.

*"That nigga can't hear me. So, relax."* Breanna chuckled.

My heart stopped, body tensed, and my mind started racing. I felt like I'd just taken a slug to my chest. Kiara had my seed. My blood? I haven't laid eyes on her since that chaotic situation that popped off during our breakup five years back, the one that left me cold towards these females. Now this bomb dropping on me in a nail shop. What the fuck?

I spotted the Vietnamese nail tech that's been working on my feet. Caught her eye and gestured for her to come over. *"Get this shit off my feet. Now."* My voice came out ice cold.

*"Yes, right away,"* she moved quick, her fingers worked fast and freed my feet.

Once done, I pulled a hundred from my pocket, dropped it in her hand for the tip. Then I laced up my black and gold Jordans real quick, adjusted my fitted and my 102 hoodie. When I stood up and turned 'round I looked dead at Constance, and all that mahogany complexion went ashy. Her usual ice queen composure cracked. I could see her searching my gaze tryin' to determine how much I'd overheard.

She stared in my eyes, and started forming words, *"Treylon..."* But before she could finish, the front door burst open. Three masked men rushed in, strapped with them thangs, scanning the room like they was hunting.

*"Everyone down!"* One shouted, waving his piece around wild.

But before anybody could move, Constance's whole demeanor switched up. She reached under her smock, pulled out a badge and heater in one smooth motion. *"FBI! Everyone stay calm!"*

The hell? My mind trying to process this shit when the back door flew open, and more agents poured in, tactical gear and everything. The nail shop turned into a warzone, people screaming, running, diving for cover.

Through the chaos, I caught Constance's eye again. This time, that soft look was gone, replaced by some cold, calculated shit. *"Mr. Taylor, we need to talk about your business ventures,"* she told me as her team took control of the niggas that tried to rob the shop.

I ain't even dignify that shit with a response. I was checkin' the nigga's that stormed in with all that heat. Tryna see if I knew any of them. Once I was fairly sure them nigga's weren't after me. I pulled my phone out and hit the panic button. Within thirty seconds, I could hear the hum of familiar V8 engines outside. My security team, Tray and the crew, rolling up heavy. They all knew better than to come in hot though. This is a chess game now, not checkers.

Constance and her team of Feds might've thought they had me, but they ain't have shit. That hoe don't even know where I lay my head at much less anything about my hustle. I don't be pillow talkin' wit' these broads so I'm

4

straight. My lawyers been preparing for this day. So, I stood my ground, cool as a fan, while Tray coordinated with my legal team through his earpiece.

*"Agent Bradley,"* my lawyer Josie Dupree-Lorion's beautiful voice came through clear on speaker. *"Unless you're formally charging my client, he's free to go. And we will be discussing this inappropriate surveillance operation of yours."*

The look on Constance's face was priceless. She knew they ain't have nothing solid. Just another alphabet agency trying to make a name off a young nigga with money. After fifteen tense minutes of them goin' back and forward, they had to let me walk.

But as I stepped out that shop, my mind wasn't on the Feds. All I could think about was Kiara and my son. My flesh and blood out there struggling? Nah, that ain't sit right wit' me. First thing first though, I had to make sure this Fed situation was handled properly. Then I'm finding my seed, consequences be damned.

Tray fell in step beside me as we headed to their trucks. *"Boss, what's the move?"* Tray asked as I opened the door to the Hellcat.

I adjusted my piece at my waist, making sure it sat right. *"Get me everything on Constance Bradley you can find without alerting the Feds. And find out if Breanna was running her mouth for real or just trying to set me up on the personal tip. If she's tryna stir up trouble with my new girl? That's one thing. If she's workin' with these pigs? That's a whole other ballgame."*

As I pulled off, I caught one last glimpse of Constance in my side mirror. Thought I knew what betrayal felt like before, but this some other level shit. Two years of moves I gotta review now, figure out what she been watching. Lucky for me Stone don't play that pillow talkin' shit. So, that hoe don't know nothing about my hustle. But first, I got a son to find.

# CHAPTER TWO THE ONE THAT GOT AWAY

Kiara Kelly wasn't just another female to me; she was the one. To be more precise the one that got away. She's the type that gets under a nigga's skin and stays there, no matter how many years pass or how many other women come through. Even now, while I'm driving down Kingston Road with my knuckles white on the steering wheel, I could still smell her coconut hair oil, still feel how perfect she fit in my arms. Real talk, she was my everything, my ride-or-die, my queen. But I fucked it up, thinking my hustle was more important than showing my woman the love she deserved.

That last argument we had. That shit haunts me more than any beef I ever had out in these streets.

"Treylon," she'd said, standing in our apartment's kitchen. Her voice was already trembling, but I was too caught up counting my paper to notice. "I been thinking..."

"What's good, baby?" I barely looked up distractedly. My whole concentration on my money.

"Nothing's good. That's what I'm trying to tell you." She wrapped her arms around herself like she used to do when she was hurting. "I'm busting my ass at nursing school, and you... you ain't ever here no more. Physically, yeah, but your mind? Your heart? That's all about the hustle now."

"Come on, K, you know I'm grinding for us. Building something solid."

"Are you though?" Her voice cracked. "When's the last time we ate dinner together? When's the last time you asked about my clinicals? Hell, when's the last time you really looked at me?"

That's when she hit me with the heavy question, tears rolling down them beautiful brown eyes.

*"What about our future, Trey? What if we had kids? Would they have to compete with your hustle too? Would they even matter to you?"*

I remember getting heated, not because she was wrong, but because deep down, I knew she was right.

*"Kiara, why you coming at me like this? Kids ain't even in the picture right now. I'm out here stacking paper, making moves. Havin' kids ain't part of the plan, understand? That shit ain't even worth discussing."*

Her face... damn. It was like I watched something die in her eyes right then. She touched her stomach so quick I almost missed it. Almost.

*"So that's really how you feel? The hustle comes before everything. Before me? Before..."* She stopped herself, wiping her tears. *"I can't do this anymore, Trey. I can't compete with the streets. Not anymore."*

But stupid me, I was too caught up in my own bullshit to hear what she wasn't saying. Too blinded by dollar signs to see she was trying to tell me something important.

*"This conversation is dead, K. You knew who I was when you got with me."* I grabbed my keys and wallet, heading for the door. *"I got moves to make."*

*"Treylon, please..."* Her voice was barely a whisper. *"Just stay. We need to talk about this."*

But I didn't stay. Didn't even look back. Just walked out that door like the fucking fool I was, thinking she'd be there when I got back. How was I supposed to know that would be the last time I'd see her? That when I came home the next day, all her stuff would be gone, leaving nothing but her vanilla scented candles and a hole in my heart that never really healed?

Now, flying down these streets with my mind racing, everything's hitting me at once. All them little signs I missed, her being sick in the mornings, the doctor's appointments she tried to tell me about, the way she kept trying to have *"serious conversations"* about our future.

Five years ago. Four whole years my son been out here without his father, all because I was too caught up in the game to see what was right in front of me. Now I got to worry about the Feds being all up in my business while tryna find my seed.

*"Fuck!"* I slammed my hand against the steering wheel, pain shooting through my knuckles. But that physical pain ain't nothing compared to the

ache in my chest, knowing what my pride cost me. Cost us. Cost my son. I was devastated.

AFTER LEAVING THAT nail shop situation with the Feds, I couldn't even focus on the road. Memories of Kiara clouding my vision and fuckin' wit' my concentration. My Hellcat Charger damn near fishtailed as I whipped onto the shoulder of Kingston Road, them 707 horses screaming against the asphalt. My chest feeling tight like I was wearing two vests instead of one. A son? My blood out here without his father? Nah, this shit can't be happenin' to me right now.

I hit Tray's line back up first, he been riding with me since we was youngins running wild in these streets.

*"Yo, I got bigger problems than them alphabet boys,"* I said, trying to keep my voice level even though my mind was hazy. *"Remember Kiara?"*

*"K? Yeah, what about her?"* Tray still sounded amped from the nail shop situation.

*"She got my son, bruh. Been raising him alone these past five years while I been out here thinking the world revolve around our paper chase."* My voice came out hoarse, betraying me. *"I need you to find her. Today. Right now. Whatever it takes."*

*"Damn, Trey..."* Tray went quiet for a minute. *"That's heavy. You sure about this intel? Especially after what just went down?"*

*"Man, I ain't never been more sure about nothing. I got a kid out there that don't even know his daddy's face. That shit ends today. Plus, we gotta handle this Fed situation ASAP."*

*"Say less, fam. I'm on it. Already got the team running background on Agent Bradley. It seems she been building a case for a minute."* Tray reported.

*"Damn, I don't like hearing that, but we should be straight. That hoe ain't never been near our setup, and she has no idea where I live. The shit I had wit' that hoe was only surface deep."* I breathed a sigh of relief and hung up.

My next call was straight to C-Lo. No point sugar coating this bullshit.

*"Speak."* C-Lo's voice had that edge he's known for.

*"We got heat, big dawg. That female I been seeing named Constance. She's FBI. Bitch just tried to set me up at the nail shop. Plus..."* I paused, the weight of everything hitting me at once.

*"I just found out K got my son and she's been raising him these past five years without me knowing."*

*"Fuck."* C-Lo went quiet for a minute. *"Stone ain't gonna like none of this. How you want to play it?"*

*"I need Tray to handle my blocks for a few weeks while I sort both situations. I got to clean up this Fed mess and find my seed. I can't have my son out here struggling while his pops getting watched by the alphabet boys."*

*"You know this don't change your responsibilities? Anything pop off, it's still on you, right?"*

*"I'm aware. Just make sure Stone knows everything, the Fed situation, my kid, all of it. I need him to understand why I'm stepping back temporarily."*

*"Understood. Watch your back. Them Feds probably got eyes everywhere now that we know about Agent Bradley."*

*"I know, and I will. But if they watchin' me umma be keepin' a low-profile on the hunt for my son. I'm ghostin' everything but that."*

*"Bet."*

I hung up and hit Carla's line next. If anybody knew where K was working at University Health, it was my nosy ass cousin.

*"What you need, Trey? I'm at work."* Carla answered already sounding irritated.

*"I need K's schedule at the hospital. What wing is she working?"*

*"K-North, 7 to 7. Why you checking for her now after five years?"*

*"It's complicated. I just found out some heavy shit. Plus, I got Feds on my ass. I need to handle both situations,"* I sighed.

*"Boy, don't you dare bring no heat around this hospital."* She paused. *"And don't fuck with K if you ain't coming correct. She's too good for your street shit."*

*"I hear ya' Carla and I'm legit. I ain't on no bullshit. I mean it. I'm even pullin' back from the grind. Tray in charge for now. My priority is findin' and makin' things right for my seed."*

*"Alright, good. I gotta go,"* she hung up.

Sitting in my Charger, watching traffic flow past, that unfamiliar feeling of fear crept up again. Not that regular street fear when a play might go wrong or when you spot them blue lights. This was deeper. What if my son rejected me? What if K wouldn't let me make it right? What if fixing this meant choosing between my freedom and my family?

My phone lit up with a text from Tray. K's address in Shreveport's south side, plus some preliminary info on Agent Bradley's investigation. My heart damn near jumped out my chest reading both. K was still local, working her dream job at University Health, while this Fed had been building a case against our operation for months.

*"I'm coming, K,"* I whispered, putting the Charger in drive. *"But first I gotta make sure these Feds don't try to take me down before I can meet my son. Umma do whatever it takes to make this shit right."*

I hit the gas, mind racing between two priorities, cleaning up this federal investigation problem and finding my kid. Time to call in every favor, use every connection. Cause one way or another, I'm fixing both these situations. My son ain't gonna grow up without a father, and these Feds ain't gonna stop me from being in his life. Not today, not ever.

# CHAPTER THREE A
# MOTHER'S HEART

T he beaming lights of Olive Garden Italian Restaurant on Youree Drive buzzed overhead as I wiped down another sticky table. My dogs were barking in the slip resistant shoes I copped from Walmart as I hurried through the last table. Five years of grinding like this, the night shift here at the restaurant and the day shift at University Health. Lord knows the extra came in handy whenever they'd let me pick up extra hours. The struggle was real, but every bit of it was worth it for my baby boy.

Treylon Jr. or TJ for short is my whole world wrapped up in one little smile. Even on nights like this, when my back is screaming at me and my feet felt like they were walking on broken glass, just thinking about them dimples in his cheeks keeps me going. That boy had his daddy's smile, and Lord, did that both warm and break my heart every single day.

I paused my cleaning and pulled out my phone to look at my lock screen and a picture of TJ from his first day of pre-K, rocking them braids I'd stayed up half the night to do, even though I had a morning shift. His gap toothed grin in that too big uniform I'd got on layaway from Walmart damn near brought tears to my eyes.

*"Baby boy, you the best thing I ever did,"* I whispered to the picture my voice shakin'.

Halloween was coming up, and TJ has been talking nonstop about being the Black Panther. I already had a payment plan set up at the costume shop, I was determined my baby wasn't gonna feel the weight of our struggle. He might not have designer kicks or the latest PlayStation like some of his classmates, but my son was loved. Deeply, completely, fiercely loved.

Some nights, when TJ's fighting them nightmares in his sleep, calling out for a daddy he ain't never met, my guilt eats me alive. In our cramped one-bedroom studio apartment, I'd watch him toss and turn, my hands clenched so tight my nails leave half-moons in my palms, wondering if keeping him from Treylon was the biggest mistake of my life.

*"Mama, why everybody else got a daddy except me?"* he asked last week, with them familiar brown eyes, his daddy's eyes, looking up at me all innocent. My heart damn near stopped beating right there.

*"Baby, you got a daddy,"* I'd told him, pulling him close while trying to keep my voice steady. *"He just... he wasn't ready when you was coming. But that don't mean you ain't loved twice as hard to make up for it. You got more love in your little finger than most folks got in their whole body."*

The buzz of my phone cut through my memories like a knife. When I saw the text message from Breanna's trifling ass, my whole world tilted sideways.

*"You won't believe what I finally told Constance stupid ass today. I told her all about Treylon Jr. So, the fact that you were keeping him a secret these five years is now out the bag. Be ready Bitch. If I can't have Treylon, I refuse to let you other bitches enjoy being with him."*

I have never understood why Breanna always wanted shit she couldn't have, and she would go to great lengths to obtain them. Her constant harassment of Treylon when we were together caused all kinds of chaos within our family. Her and her mother are just alike so she would uphold Breanna and all her bullshit no matter how grimy it was or who she crossed.

My legs went weak, hands shaking so bad the phone nearly slipped from my grip. I had to sit down in one of the sticky booths I just cleaned. Treylon knew. After all these years of protecting our son, of carrying this weight alone, of crying myself to sleep some nights missing him so bad it physically hurt... he knew.

*"Shit, shit, shit,"* I whispered, my heart racing.

Before I could even process what this meant, my phone lit up again. It was Carla calling. I answered with shaky fingers.

*"K, where you at?"* Carla's voice was urgent.

*"Work. What's wrong?"*

*"Listen, Trey's looking for you. He knows everything about TJ, where you work, probably where you stay by now."* She paused. *"He's different now, K. When*

*he asked about you today... girl, I ain't never heard him sound like that. Like he regrets everything that went down five years ago when you tried telling him about the baby."*

*"What am I supposed to do, Carla? He's gonna be mad—"* I asked my chest tight like somebody was sitting on it.

*"Girl, stop. You remember how he was before all that street shit got heavy? How he used to talk about wanting a family someday? That's the Trey I heard today. Not the one who was too caught up in his hustle to listen five years ago."*

I wiped my eyes with my free hand, remembering the young Treylon who used to dream bigger than just running blocks.

*"You think... you think he really wants to be in TJ's life?"*

*"K, that man looked shook to his core when he found out. Like his whole world just flipped upside down. He's making calls, pulling back from the streets. Shit, he's even got Tray handling his business while he figures this out."*

*"For real?"* Something in my chest loosened just a little.

*"Girl, yes. And look, I know you're scared. But maybe... maybe this is the chance for TJ to have what you always wanted for him. His daddy. His whole family. The three of y'all together."*

I closed my eyes, thinking about all them times TJ woke up crying from nightmares, begging for a daddy he ain't never met. My hands still shaking, but for a different reason now. It feels like maybe they are shaking with hope instead of just fear.

*"What if he hates me for keeping this from him?"* My voice was barely above a whisper.

*"K, that man could never hate you. Mad? Probably. Hurt? For sure. But hate? Nah. Not the way he was talking today."* Carla's voice went soft. *"Plus, once he sees that baby boy... girl, it's over. TJ got his whole face."*

For the first time since reading Breanna's text, I felt something besides panic. Maybe, just maybe, this was God's way of fixing what broke five years ago. Maybe it was time for TJ to know his daddy, and for his daddy to know him.

*"I gotta go get my baby from Miss Jenkins,"* I said, standing up on legs that felt like Jell-O. *"And Carla? Thank you."*

*"Just remember, you've raised that boy right, by yourself, working two jobs and never complained. You're strong as hell, K. Whatever comes next, you got this. And you got me."*

I clocked out early, telling Sasha I wasn't feeling well. The whole walk to my beat-up Honda, I was scared but excited. I jumped in and gunned the engine speeding out the lot. Once on the road I kept checking the rearview, half expecting to see that familiar Charger pulling up behind me. This time though, the thought didn't just bring fear. It brought something else too, something that felt a whole lot like hope.

*"Lord,"* I whispered, gripping my steering wheel tight, *"if you listening, please let this be the beginning of something good. Please let my baby finally have his daddy. Please let Treylon understand why I did what I did. And please... please let us be a family."*

Because truth was, even after five years, the eyes I saw every day in our son's face still had the power to make my heart skip beats. And maybe, just maybe, it was time to face them again and not just in TJ's sweet face, but in his daddy's too.

The long drive home kept me on edge. Despite my conversation with Carla, doubts creep in. Fear and anxiety warring within. What was I supposed to do if Carla was wrong? Treylon wasn't the type to let something like this slide. I remember how he moved in the streets and he was focused, determined, unstoppable when he wanted something. And this wasn't about some hustle or territory beef he was dealin' with. This was about his son. Our son.

My mind was spinning with a thousand thoughts at once. Would he be mad that I'd kept this from him? Would he try to take TJ? Would he even want to be involved, or would he just pop in and out of TJ's life, leaving our baby boy with the same kind of hurt and pain I grew up with?

But deep down, past all that fear and anxiety, there was this tiny part of my heart that felt... relief. Like maybe I didn't have to carry this load by myself no more. Like maybe, just maybe, my baby boy could know his daddy after all.

When I made it home my hands were trembling so bad I could barely get my key in the door of the apartment.

Miss Jenkins from next door was watching TJ, like she did most nights I had to work late. Through the thin walls, I could hear my baby's laugh mixing with the sound of cartoons.

Taking a deep breath, I straightened my uniform and fixed my face. Whatever storm was coming, I had to be strong for TJ. That boy is my heart walking around outside my body, and no matter what went down with Treylon, protecting TJ's heart was all that mattered.

But damn if my own heart wasn't breaking all over again, thinking about facing them eyes I'd never quite managed to forget. *"Shit, how could I when I had a miniature version of him walkin' around everyday lookin' at me with an identical pair?"*

# CHAPTER FOUR TJ'S
# SCARY NIGHTMARES

TJ perched on the edge of his twin bed, his small hands gripping his Black Panther blanket like it was his last line of defense. Moonlight crept through them dollar store curtains, throwing shadows that danced like demons on the walls. Every night, like clockwork, the same fear would creep up. The cold sweats. The voices. The straight terror.

Sleep was TJ's enemy. While other kids dreamed about superheroes and candy, his dreams was dark places where shadows had faces and monsters lurked under his bed. Ghosts floated in the corners of his mind, witches laughed from somewhere up high, and creatures with faces twisted like pretzels slithered out from places they ain't have no business being.

*"Daddy,"* TJ's voice barely a whisper in the dark room, trembling like autumn leaves, *"please come back. Please come get me."*

His daddy been gone his whole life. TJ ain't fully understand why—mama always talking in them soft, sad tones about him *"not being ready."* But in his four-year-old heart, TJ believed his daddy was the only one who could chase the monsters away. Mama always said his daddy was the strongest, the bravest. So, in TJ's mind, if his daddy was here, them nightmares wouldn't dare show their faces.

TJ squeezed his eyes shut, praying tonight would be different. Maybe his daddy would come through, scoop him up with them strong arms mama always talked about, and make all the bad stuff disappear. But soon as sleep grabbed hold, the nightmare slid in.

He was in some dark park now, trees looking like they was throwing up gang signs with their twisted branches. Wind howling through the playground equipment sounded like them spirits mama warned him about.

The ghosts came first, pale figures floating silent, their empty eyes locked on TJ. Then them witches showed up, cackling like they just heard the world's meanest joke, circling him from above.

*"Daddy!"* TJ's scream echoed through the empty playground.

The ground started shaking like a bass system in a Charger, and from the darkness came the worst one, some creature with eyes red as blood and teeth sharp as razors, crawling toward him like something out the horror movie he snuck and watch. Ever since he watched *"Vampires,"* he's been having bad dreams.

*"Ain't nobody here for you,"* it growled.

*"No! My daddy coming!"* TJ cried, but his words sounded weak.

*"TJ! Baby, wake up!"* Mama's voice cut through the darkness, her hands shaking him cautiously. *"Mama's here, baby. Mama got you."*

TJ's eyes snapped open, tears streaming down his face. He launched himself into Kiara's arms, his little body shaking hard.

*"The monsters, Mama,"* he sobbed. *"They keep coming back. I need my daddy. Where my daddy at? Why he ain't here to protect me?"*

Kiara held her baby close, her own tears falling silent on his braids. Her heart feeling like somebody done took a sledgehammer to it, watching her son battle demons she couldn't fight for him.

*"Lord,"* she prayed silently, while rocking TJ back and forth, *"I know I messed up. I know I should've tried harder to tell Treylon. But please, please don't let my baby suffer for my choices. Please send his daddy to him. Treylon always knew how to make everything feel safe, feel right. My baby needs that now more than ever."*

TJ's sobs slowly quieted to hiccups, but his grip on Kiara's nightshirt stayed tight. *"Mama,"* he whispered, *"you think my daddy ever think about me?"*

Kiara's guilt hit her hard. Here she was, knowing Treylon was out there right now, probably turning the city upside down looking for them, while their baby crying out for him every night.

*"Baby,"* she whispered, stroking his back, *"your daddy... he gonna be here soon. Mama promise you that. And when he get here, ain't no monster, no ghost, no nothing gonna dare mess with you ever again."*

TJ pulled back, them familiar brown eyes, Treylon's eyes looking up at her all hopeful.

*"For real, Mama? Daddy's coming?"*

*"Yeah, baby,"* Kiara said, her voice stronger now. *"Your daddy coming. And when he get here, all them bad dreams gonna have to catch the fade. 'Cause ain't nothing in this world, not no ghost, not no monster, nor nothing is stronger than your daddy when he's protecting what's his."*

TJ finally settled back against his pillows, clutching his stuffed bear.

*"You think Daddy brave enough to fight all the monsters, Mama?"*

*"Baby boy,"* Kiara whispered, tucking him in tight, *"your daddy is the bravest man I've ever known. Them monsters ain't ready for what's coming."*

Sitting there in the dark, watching her son finally drift back to peaceful sleep, Kiara let her tears fall free. *"Treylon,"* she whispered to the empty room, *"wherever you're at right now, whatever you're thinking about me keeping him from you... just know your son needs you. He been needing you. Please come find us. Come chase away his monsters like you used to chase away mine."*

'Cause truth was, them nightmares wasn't just haunting TJ. They was hunting Kiara too, nightmares of regret, of guilt, of four years of watching their baby boy cry out for a daddy she kept in the shadows. But maybe, just maybe, it wasn't too late to make it right.

# CHAPTER FIVE FACE TO FACE

As soon as Tray hit my line with Kiara's address, my whole world shifted. River Oaks Apartments on Bert Kouns Industrial Loop, she lived about twenty minutes from my spot. My hands was trembling when I punched that shit into my GPS, but I made myself wait. I had to get my head straight first.

I hit up my lawyer Josie before making any moves. She pulled up to my spot looking stressed, wit' them designer heels clicking against my marble floors.

"*Treylon, the situation with this FBI case is serious,*" Josie said, spreading files across my kitchen island. "*Agent Bradley's been building this case for months. We got surveillance photos, wire taps, CI statements—*"

"*How bad we talking?*" I asked, my stomach knotting up.

"*Ten to fifteen if they can prove everything they claim. Stone's operation is their main target, but you're high on their list.*" She pushed her glasses up, fixing me with that look I paid her big money for. "*You need to disappear for a while. Cut all contact with Stone and let Tray handle everything going forward. Any communication between you two could give them what they need. We already know they don't have anything tangible or they woulda took you in on the spot. Stone runs a tight ship so he ain't got no leaks.*"

"*And what about my son? I just found out about him, I can't just—*" My fists clenched in my frustration.

"*That's actually your best play right now,*" Josie cut in. "*You being a present father, getting legitimate income, and showing family ties to the community. It all helps if this goes to court. But you gotta cut them street ties. Cut them off clean Treylon. Your only saving grace is you don't have a criminal record.*"

The irony wasn't lost on me. I finally found out about my seed, but the streets might cost me the chance to be his father.

*"How long are we talking 'bout?"*

*"Six months minimum. Let's give the investigation time to cool off. Meanwhile, we'll work on your defense strategy."* She paused. *"But Treylon, I'm serious. One wrong move, one meeting with Stone, and you could miss your son's whole childhood."*

The thought of that gave me a strange feeling in my chest. While Mrs Lorion packed up her briefcase, my mind was spinning. How am I supposed to be able to focus on beating a federal case when all I can think about is the five years I already missed with my son?

I spent that whole morning pacing my crib like a caged animal, watching Halloween decorations go up across the street. Little kids running around hyped about trick-or-treating tomorrow, and somewhere out there, my own son probably had his costume ready. My son. Them words still felt strange in my mouth, like speaking a language I should've known but never learned.

*"You sure about this location?"* I called Tray again, needed to be certain.

*"Yeah, boss. K got a one-bedroom studio apartment. The number is 247. She been working two jobs with a night shift at Olive Garden Restaurant and a day shift at University Health. She living clean, keeping y'alls son in a good school district. She ain't playing 'bout his future."*

That knowledge hit me in the chest. While I been out here flooding these streets with product, she been holding it down alone, making sure our boy had a shot at something better.

My connect in the apartment office said her rent was always on time, but sometimes just barely. Said she stayed to herself, worked hard, kept that boy looking clean and proper. Pride and shame warred in my chest, pride that she was such a good mama, shame that I hadn't been there to make it easier.

By evening, I couldn't wait no more. I grabbed the keys to my Charger and checked my reflection in the hallway mirror. I had to look right for this. I switched out my usual street clothes for some clean dark jeans and a black button-up. I needed to look like somebody's father, not just another hustler.

Rolling through them streets, my mind was going a hundred different directions. What my son look like? Does he have my eyes? My smile? Is he smart like his mama? Did he play sports? What's his favorite color? Every question I should've been asking for five years hit me all at once.

Pulling into River Oaks, I scoped the scene proper. Nice enough spot, clean, quiet, security cameras at the gates. Kiara picked somewhere safe for our boy. Our boy. Damn.

My palms was sweating on the steering wheel as I parked. Through a ground floor window, I could see Halloween decorations and kids running around. Somewhere in one of these units, my son was probably doing the same thing.

Standing outside apartment 247, everything in me was at war. Part of me wanted to kick the door down, demand answers about why she kept my seed from me. Another part wanted to drop to my knees and beg forgiveness for being the kind of man she couldn't trust with the truth. And deep down, past all that anger and guilt, there was this hope I ain't felt in years. Hope that maybe I can fix what I broke. Hope that despite the Feds watching my every move, despite having to choose between the streets and my family, it wasn't too late to be the man they both deserved.

My heart still jumped thinking 'bout seeing K in them scrubs she'd be wearin' at University Health. Five years ain't dimmed none of what I felt for her. If anything, knowing she raised our son alone, kept grinding no matter what, made me love her more. The way she protected our boy, made sure he had everything he needed, that's the kind of love you can't fake.

I raised my hand to knock, then stopped. Through the door, I could hear a kid laughing at something on TV. My son's laugh. My heart damn near stopped right there.

When I finally knocked, the three seconds before the door opened felt like three lifetimes. Then there she was, Kiara. Still beautiful enough to stop traffic, but with this tiredness around her eyes that wasn't there before. Her nurse's scrubs had Halloween pumpkins on them, probably for the kids at the hospital. She still wore that coconut-scented hair oil I used to love.

Our eyes locked, and five years of loving her, missing her, regretting every choice that led to this moment hit me like a physical blow. But this wasn't about us, at least not yet. This was about the truth she'd been carrying alone for too long.

"Kiara," I said, trying to keep my voice steady even though my heart was trying to escape my chest. "We need to talk."

She gripped the doorframe like she needed it to stand. "Treylon, I—"

"I know," I cut her off, my voice barely above a whisper. "I know about my son."

Behind her, I caught a glimpse of little boy shoes by the door and a cartoon backpack hung on a hook. Evidence of the life I should've been part of all along. The life I was here to claim, even if it meant walking away from everything else.

Because this wasn't just about meeting my son or beating them federal charges. This was about making my family whole again. About being the man K always believed I could be, before the streets got their hooks in me. About giving my son the father he deserved, even if it meant losing everything else I built.

Whatever it took. However long it took. My family was worth more than any hustle.

# CHAPTER SIX A FATHER'S HEART

Stepping into that apartment felt surreal. The whole spot smelled like fresh baked cookies and that vanilla scent K always loved. Halloween paper chains hung from the ceiling, probably made by little hands. My son's hands. Photos lined the walls of my boy's whole life laid out in frames I should've been in.

Then I heard it, that laugh comin' from the back room. High and sweet, just like K's, but with something of my own voice in it too. My legs damn near gave out right there.

K stood in front of me looking like every dream I had these past five years, but with this new strength in her shoulders. Mama bear strength. Her eyes were doing that thing they used to do when she was trying not to cry, and it took everything in me not to reach for her like I used to.

*"Look,"* she started, her voice shaking. *"I know you probably hate me right now—"*

*"Hate you?"* My laugh came out bitter. *"K, I been loving you all this whole time. Even when I was too stupid to show it right."*

She wrapped her arms around herself, defensive. *"You said you ain't want no kids, Trey. Said it wasn't in your plans. What was I supposed to do?"*

*"You was supposed to trust me!"* The words came out louder than I meant, and we both glanced toward the back room. I lowered my voice but couldn't hide the heat in it. *"You was supposed to give me a chance to step up, to be better than what I was showing you. Instead, you just... disappeared. Took my son and bounced without a word."*

*"Your son?"* Her eyes flashed fire like they used to when we'd argue. *"Where was all this energy about 'your son' when I was trying to tell you I was pregnant?*

23

*When I was dropping hints about doctor's appointments? When I was straight up asking you about our future?"* She stepped closer, jabbing her finger in my chest. *"You was too busy counting money to count the signs, Treylon. Too caught up in them streets to see what was right in front of you."*

*"And now?"* I caught her hand before she could pull it back, held it against my chest where my heart was beating wild. *"What about now, K? You feel this? This heart ain't beat right since you left. And now I find out I got a whole son out here. That I missed his first words, first steps, first everything."*

Before she could answer, I heard them little footsteps comin' down the hall. Time slowed down as my boy, my son, appeared around the corner. Looking at him was like looking in a mirror to my past. He had my eyes, my nose, my chin, but K's soft features, her gentle spirit showing in how he held himself.

*"TJ,"* K said soft, *"baby, this is... this is your daddy."*

His big brown eyes, my eyes, looked up at me curious but cautious. He was rocking a Black Panther t-shirt, looking fresh in some little Jordans that matched mine.

*"You my real daddy?"* He asked, his voice small but steady. *"The one Mama said wasn't ready before?"*

I dropped down to one knee, getting on his level. *"Yeah, little man. I'm your daddy. And I know I'm late, but I'm ready now. I been waiting my whole life to meet you, even when I ain't know it."*

He studied me serious, then pointed at my shoes.

*"We got the same shoes."*

*"Yeah, we do."* I smiled, feeling tears trying to come. *"I hear you gonna be Black Panther for Halloween tomorrow?"*

His whole face lit up. *"Wakanda Forever!"* He did the crossed arms thing, and my heart damn near exploded.

The two of us ended up sitting on the floor, him showing me his action figures, telling me about school, about his friends. Then his voice got quiet.

*"Daddy... you gonna stay? For real?"*

*"For real for real, little man."* I pulled him close, breathing in that baby shampoo smell. *"I ain't going nowhere."*

*"Good."* He leaned into me like he'd been waiting his whole life to do it. *"Cause I get bad dreams sometimes. Mama tries to help, but..."*

*"Tell me about these dreams, son. We'll see what I can do."* The word son felt right on my tongue.

He told me about the monsters, the shadows, how scared he got at night. With every word, my heart broke and healed at the same time.

*"Listen here, TJ,"* I said, holding his little face in my hands. *"Ain't nothing, no monster, no shadow, nothing, gonna hurt you ever again. Daddy's here now. For good."*

Later, after K put him to bed, we sat at her little kitchen table. It was time for me to face a different kind of monster.

*"K, I gotta tell you something."* I explained about the Feds, about Constance being undercover, about stepping back from the streets. When I mentioned Breanna's involvement, her face went hard.

*"That snake been trying to destroy lives since we was kids,"* she spat. *"Now she might take my son's father away right after he found him?"*

*"Nah. I ain't letting that happen."* I reached across the table and took her hand. *"My lawyer's handling it. I'm done with all that for a while anyway. Got something way more important to focus on right now."*

*"What if they lock you up, Trey?"* Her voice cracked. *"What if TJ loses you right after finding you? He'd be devastated."*

*"Then I'll write him every day. Call him every chance I get. Love him so hard through them walls he'll feel it in his sleep."* I squeezed her hand. *"But they gotta catch me first. And right now, I'm just a father trying to do right by his son."*

*"I'm scared, Trey. For all of us."* K wiped her eyes.

*"Me too, baby."* I pulled her into my arms, feeling her melt against me like no time had passed. *"But we stronger together. Always was."*

We sat there holding each other, listening to our son's soft breathing from the other room. Tomorrow I'd face them federal charges. Tomorrow I'd deal with Breanna's betrayal. Tomorrow I'd figure out how to be the father my son deserved.

WALKING INTO MY CRIB after leaving K and TJ felt strange when I saw three silhouettes posted up in my living room. Zaylar Stone Crewens sitting in my favorite leather recliner with Cree C-Lo Logan and Myron Dax flanking him like dark angels was alarming to the extreme. The only light coming from my custom fish tank, making their faces look like something out of a horror flick.

*"Trey,"* Stone's smooth voice rang out, *"I hear you had quite the day."*

My hand twitched toward my piece before I caught myself. These were my people, even if the scene looked like something about to go left.

*"Stone,"* I kept my voice respectful but firm, *"I wasn't expecting company."*

*"Clearly."* C-Lo's platinum grill caught the blue light from the tank. *"But certain conversations can't wait, ya' feel me?"*

I nodded.

*"C-Lo filled me in about Agent Bradley and your family situation. Messy business when family turns snake."* Stone gestured to the couch across from him. *"Take a seat, Trey. We need to discuss your future."*

Sinking into the couch across from them, I kept my guard up. Stone makin' a house call is never a good thing.

*"Breanna Wilson is K's own blood cousin. If she's the one that set this whole thing in motion and got the Feds watching me, on some spiteful snake shit. I'mma kill that hoe."*

*"Blood ain't always loyal,"* C-Lo shook his head. *"When you hit my line earlier about the Fed situation, I already knew it was deeper than just business. Breanna been trying to slide between you and K since way back when, right?"*

*"Since me and K was first together,"* I confirmed. *"Her own cousin, and she been plotting the whole time. Now she done brought the alphabet boys to our door and exposed my son just to be messy."*

Stone leaned forward, his marble gray eyes glinting in the darkness.

*"Family's supposed to protect family. What she did... that's beyond street beef. That's blood betrayal."*

*"And now my son..."* I had to pause, get my emotions in check. *"My boy finally got his daddy in his life, and this situation might take me away from him."*

*"Not gonna happen."* Stone nodded to Myron, who pulled out a folder thick as a Bible. *"See, when C-Lo brought me what you told him about the Feds and Agent Bradley, we already had a plan in motion. Been watching them watch you. And now we got something better than a plan, we got a new future for you."*

*"What are you saying?"* My throat went dry.

*"I'm saying,"* Stone's smile was both warm and dangerous, *"that Key Stone Construction is 'bout to hire their new crew chief. Starting salary 75K, with full benefits, plus 401K and you'll have regular working man hours, of 9 to 5, Monday through Friday."*

"Stone, I..." My mind was spinning trying to catch up.

*"Let me finish."* He held up a hand. *"Ya' see, you been loyal. Made us both a lot of money. But every king gotta know when to change the game. Sometimes that means protecting your pieces by moving them off the board. But more importantly this is about family. Real family. The kind that look out for each other no matter what."*

C-Lo stepped forward, the gators on his feet silent on my carpet. *"The job comes with all the proper paperwork. W2s, tax records, everything's clean. As far as the worlds concerned, you been working construction management since you got out the military."*

*"The military?"* I raised an eyebrow.

Myron spoke up, his voice gravelly. *"Four years Army Corps of Engineers. Honorable discharge. I got the documents right here; they look realer than the real ones."*

*"Why?"* The question came out before I could stop it. *"Why go through all this?"*

Stone stood up, his 6'3" frame casting a shadow over me. *"Because loyalty goes both ways, Trey. You helped build this empire. Now we helping you build something that can't get took by no Fed."* He put a heavy hand on my shoulder. *"Plus, ain't no real man gonna stand in the way of another man taking care of his seed."*

*"What's the catch?"* I had to ask.

*"The catch is that you actually gotta work the job."* C-Lo grinned. *"For real for real. Learn the business from the ground up. 'Cause Key Stone Construction ain't just a front, it's our future. Legal money hit different when you got a family to feed."*

*"Your crew chief position gonna be handling our southwest projects,"* Myron added. *"Managing twenty men, overseeing four active sites. Real responsibility, real work."*

*"And them Feds?"* I asked.

Stone's laugh was deep. *"Let them watch you swing a hammer, read blueprints, make honest money. Best cover is the truth. Ya' feel me? A year from now, Agent Bradley gonna be looking real stupid trying to prove you are anything but a working man trying to do right by his family."*

I sat there taking it all in. *"This real? Just like that?"*

*"Just like that."* Stone's voice went serious. *"But understand something, this ain't no temporary move. This is your life now. You choosing this path, you on it for good. No straddling fences, no side plays. You feel me?"*

*"I feel you."* I stood up, looked each man in the eye. *"I appreciate this. For real."*

*"Show us by being the father that boy deserves,"* Stone said. *"And by being the man your lady needs you to be. By building something that can't get took by no cage or bullet."*

*"One more thing,"* C-Lo added. *"Breanna Wilson. We handling that situation in house. Far as you are concerned, that chapter is closed."*

*"But—"* I started to protest.

*"But nothing,"* Stone's voice went cold. *"Family handle family business. You got a new family to focus on. Let us deal with the snake."*

They left like shadows, leaving nothing but that folder and a set of keys to a company truck. Looking at them keys, feeling their weight, I knew my whole world just shifted again.

My phone buzzed, and I opened the text to see a picture from K of TJ sleeping peaceful. *"No nightmares tonight,"* the text read.

*"Thank you,"* I whispered to my empty living room, knowing Stone probably had ears somewhere still listening. Because that's what real family does, they hear you even when you ain't speaking out loud.

Tomorrow I'd start my new life. Learning how to read blueprints instead of counting bands. Wearing a hard hat instead of watching my back. Building houses instead of trapping out of them.

And for the first time since I could remember, I was actually looking forward to punching a clock. 'Cause now I had something real to work for, something that couldn't get took by no Fed, no snitch, and no bullet.

I had my family. And thanks to Stone, I had a way to keep them.

# CHAPTER SEVEN TJ'S FIRST FAMILY SHOPPING TRIP

Standing outside Spirit Halloween the next morning, my whole world was wrapped around them tiny fingers holding mine. TJ was like looking in a time machine. He has the same high cheekbones my pops had and gave to me. The same eyes that look right through you too. He even has that little swag in his walk that K claims is pure Taylor blood. In every way he is my mini me and I'm as proud as can be.

The morning light seemed to shine brighter today. Maybe 'cause for the first time in forever, I wasn't thinking about re-ups or territory or staying ahead of the competition. My whole focus was on this little king holding my hand, rocking them fresh J's I copped him last night after K finally let me stay long enough to really talk and find out what he likes.

"Daddy!" TJ tugged on my hand his big brown eyes sparkling. *"Look at the vampire costume! It got real fangs and everything!"*

That word, 'Daddy' hit me in the chest every time he said it. It ain't been 24 hours since I found out about him, and already this little man had my whole heart on lock.

*"You sure that's what you want, little man?"* I knelt down to his level, something I started doin' last night. *"I thought you was set on being Black Panther? Wakanda Forever and all that?"*

He leaned in close, his voice dropping to what he probably thought was a whisper but was really just his regular voice with extra breath.

*"Remember what I told you 'bout them dreams? The scary ones?"*

I swallowed hard. My chest tightened. My son was having nightmares and I wasn't there to chase them away.

*"Yeah, I remember, TJ."*

*"Well, if I'm a scary vampire, then nothing else scary can get me."*

His little face was so serious, trying to solve his problems the best way his four-year-old mind could figure out. Smart like his mama, no doubt.

I pulled him closer, breathing in that baby shampoo smell K still used on him.

*"Listen here, little king. Ain't nothing, not no monsters, no witches, or no bad dreams gonna touch you. You know why?"*

He shook his head; the fresh braids K did this morning swaying.

*"Cause your daddy's here now. And ain't nothing getting past me to hurt my son. Nothing."* I meant every word with my whole soul. *"So, you pick whatever costume makes you happy. Black Panther, vampire, whatever you want. The scary stuff? That's my job to handle. Understand?"*

He nodded, his big brown eyes full of trust. He might not never know it, but that one gesture of belief in me went a long way towards soothing my fears. Fears that I'm too late to earn his trust. Too late to make a difference in his life.

K was watching us, trying to look cool but I could see the tears she was strugglin' to hold back. She always did wear her heart in her eyes. It made it impossible for me to forget her, even when I was trying my hardest to move on.

When TJ ran off to check out some skeleton display, K stepped closer, her voice low.

*"He really does love having you here, Trey. It's like... like something in him knew his daddy was coming."*

I took a deep breath, knowing it was time.

*"K, I need to tell you something. It's about my new situation."*

She tensed up, probably thinking I was 'bout to say some street shit. *"Trey..."*

*"Nah, listen. Stone came to see me last night. After I left y'all."* I kept my voice quiet, my eyes on TJ while he explored the store. *"I'm working at Key Stone Construction now. For real for real. Crew chief position, benefits, 401K, everything legit. Nine to five, Monday through Friday."*

*"What? How..."* Her eyes went wide.

*"Stone arranged it. A clean break from everything in the streets. He said loyalty goes both ways, and it was time for me to build something that can't get took."* I reached for her hand, and damn if she didn't let me take it. *"I'm done*

with the old life, K. Completely. This ain't temporary, ain't no front. This my real job now."

"You serious?" Her voice shook a little. "Just like that?"

"Just like that. 'Cause this," I nodded toward TJ, who was now trying on a ninja mask, "this right here is worth more than any hustle. You're worth more. Our family's worth more."

"Family?" She whispered it like she was scared to believe.

"If you'll let me, K. I know I got years to make up for, trust to rebuild. But I'm ready to do whatever it takes to be the father TJ deserves, and the man you always seen in me before I even saw it myself."

"What about the Feds? The investigation?" She wiped a tear quick, trying to play it cool.

"Let them watch me swing a hammer and read blueprints on the job. The best cover is the truth, and truth is, I'm just trying to take care of my family now." I squeezed her hand. "No more looking over our shoulders, no more wondering if I'm gonna come home at night. I'll just be on regular working man hours and family time from now on."

"Daddy!" TJ came running back with both costumes plus that ninja fit. "Can I try them all on?"

"Get all three, little man." I scooped him up onto my shoulders. "Whatever you want. Your daddy got you."

"Forever?" he asked, them little hands holding my head.

"Forever and a day, son." I caught K's eye, seeing that hope she was trying to hold back. "Both of you. I'm building something real this time. Something that's gonna last."

Later, watching TJ model all three costumes while K helped him with the masks and capes, I knew Stone was right. This is what real power looks like, not running blocks or stacking paper, but building a future the Feds can't touch. A future where my son never gotta wonder if his daddy love the streets more than him. Where my queen never gotta hold down everything alone again.

"K," I said soft, while TJ was changing into the next costume. "I love y'all. Both of y'all. And I'm gonna prove it every day from here on out."

"We love you too, Trey. Just... don't disappear on us again," she smiled that real smile I missed so bad, the one that always made my heart skip a beat.

*"Never."* I pulled her close, breathing in that coconut smell I could never forget. *"This my life now. Y'all my life now. Everything else is just background noise."*

And standing there in Spirit Halloween, holding my queen while our son played superhero, I finally felt like a real man. Cause real men don't build empires, they build families.

# CHAPTER EIGHT
# CREATING FAMILY
# MEMORIES

The apartment glowed with candlelight from our freshly carved pumpkins, making shadows dance across the walls. TJ had insisted on carving his pumpkin to look like some anime character I ain't never heard of, but Treylon jumped right in like he knew exactly what our baby was talking about. Watching them together, heads bent over that pumpkin, my heart felt so full it hurt.

*"Daddy, did you know Naruto can make shadow clones?"* TJ's eyes were bright with excitement as he scooped seeds into the bowl I'd set out.

*"That means he can make copies of himself and fight all the bad guys at once!"*

*"For real?"* Treylon's whole face lit up when TJ spoke, like every word our son said was pure gold. *"That's some smart thinking right there. Bet nobody can beat him when he do that, huh?"*

Looking at them both covered in pumpkin guts, something in my chest twisted. Four years of moments like this, stolen from both of them. The guilt hit fresh, making my hands shake as I wiped down the kitchen counter.

Treylon must've noticed 'cause he caught my eye across the room. He still could read me like a book, even after all this time. *"Hey TJ, why don't you go wash your hands and get them Halloween movies you was telling me about? We can watch one before bed."*

As soon as our son bounced off to his room, Treylon was beside me, close enough I could smell that same Creed cologne he always wore. Some things just don't change.

*"Talk to me, K,"* he said softly. *"What's going on in that beautiful head of yours?"*

Before I could answer, his phone started buzzing. He checked the screen and his whole body tensed up.

*"It's my lawyer,"* he said, voice tight. *"I gotta take this."*

I nodded, watching him step into the kitchen. Even from where I stood, I could hear his voice change when he answered and his street voice came back just a little.

*"Josie? What's good?"*

Then his whole demeanor shifted. I watched his shoulders relax, saw that smile start spreading across his face.

*"You serious? Just like that?"* He ran a hand over his face. *"Nah, nah, I hear you. Because she what?"* He let out a low whistle. *"Damn. Whole case dismissed? Bet."* He was quiet for a minute. *"Good looking out, Josie. Yeah, I'm with them now. Bet. Tomorrow."*

When he turned back to me, he was grinning hard. I like the sight 'cause I ain't seen that smile in years.

*"The case was dismissed,"* he said, pulling me close. *"That Fed, Constance, she messed up. Told her supervisors about getting involved with me personally. Made everything she found invalid. Judge threw the whole thing out."*

*"For real?"* My voice shook. *"Just like that?"*

*"Just like that. I have a clean slate, baby."* His hands framed my face. *"Now let me finish what I was trying to say before. I have been missing you something fierce, K. Not just cause of TJ, though that boy make me wanna be better every second. But because you..."* He shook his head. *"You always was the best part of me."*

*"Trey..."* My heart was doing flips.

*"Listen. Everything's different now. I got my legit job at Key Stone, the case is dismissed, and nothing's hanging over our heads. Let me love you right this time? Let me be the man you always knew I could be?"* He asked.

*"I'm scared,"* I whispered, keeping it real. *"What if..."*

*"No what ifs. I'm here. For real this time."* His thumb brushed my cheek. *"The streets can't have me no more. My hearts too full of y'all to have room for that life."*

Before I could respond, TJ came running back in with his DVDs. *"Found them! Can we watch Ghostbusters first?"*

Trey stepped back, but his eyes stayed locked on mine. *"Whatever you want, little man. Tonight's about family."*

That word, family, hung between us as we settled on the couch. TJ curled up in the middle like he'd been doing it forever, head on his daddy's chest, feet in my lap. The movie started playing but I barely saw it.

Instead, I watched Trey explain the funny parts to our son, saw how affectionate his hands were when he fixed TJ's blanket, noticed how he kept glancing at me like he couldn't quite believe we was all really here. The street king was gone, replaced by something better, a father, a man ready to love us right.

That old fear still tried to creep in, but then Trey reached across the back of the couch, his fingers finding mine in the dark. And just like that, I was nineteen again, falling in love with my first everything. Only now we had this beautiful boy between us, this second chance to be the family we was always meant to be.

*"We gone be alright,"* he whispered, squeezing my hand. *"I got my job, got my freedom, got my family. There ain't nothing else I need."*

Watching him hold our sleeping son, seeing that peace in his eyes, I finally believed him. Some things worth taking a chance on. Some loves worth fighting for. And this right here? This was everything.

*"I love you too,"* I whispered back. *"Both of you."*

His smile in the TV light was pure joy. *"I love you more, baby. And this time, I'm doing everything right. Building our future brick by brick, no shortcuts, no games. Just us."*

And sitting there in the soft glow of carved pumpkins and family movies, I felt whole for the first time in five years. My son had his daddy. My heart had its home. And our future? It was finally looking as bright as the candles dancing on the walls.

# CHAPTER NINE
# TREYLON'S NEW PATH

The sun wasn't even up when I rolled into Key Stone Construction's main yard. I traded in my designer fits for steel-toe Timbs and heavy Carhartt work gear. It felt strange at first, but something about it felt right too, wearing honest work clothes for my new honest life.

Andy Givens, the veteran crew chief Stone set me up with, was already there, coffee in one hand, iPad in the other. Nigga looked like he been building since they invented hammers.

*"Treylon Taylor?"* He asked extending a weathered hand. *"Welcome to the legitimate hustle, young blood. Stone said you was coming."*

*"Appreciate you showing me the ropes,"* I said, matching his firm grip.

*"First things first, safety gear."* Andy led me to a storage container that looked as organized as a pharmacy. *"Hard hat ain't optional, ever. Don't care if you just walking through to check progress. OSHA ain't playing, and neither am I."*

He handed me a white hard hat with the Key Stone logo. *"White means management. You earn them stickers that go on it, each one represent different certifications."*

*"Them designer clothes you probably used to? Leave 'em at home. This about function, not fashion. Boots always steel-toe, pants always heavy duty. One wrong move with a power tool will teach you quick why we serious about this."* Next came the vest, safety glasses, work gloves.

For the next few hours, Andy ran down everything, site management software on the iPad, daily safety meetings, progress reports, dealing with inspectors, managing subcontractors.

*"The most important part of your job is keeping them twenty men under you alive and working efficiently."* He pulled up some blueprints. *"You gotta know*

*every detail of these plans. What the plumbers doing affect what the electricians can do. What the framers doing affect everybody. It's like chess, but with people's lives and millions of dollars on the line."*

By lunch, my head was spinning with codes, regulations, and procedures. But unlike my old life, everything here was straight forward. No looking over my shoulder, no hidden meanings. Just honest work building something real.

*"You got a family?"* Andy asked while we checked foundation measurements.

*"Yeah,"* I couldn't help smiling. *"A son and his mama. Finally doing right by them."*

*"Good. Keep that picture in your head when this job get tough. Cause it will."* He marked something on his iPad. *"But ain't nothing better than building something your kid can point to and say, 'my daddy built that.'"*

By the end of the day, I was tired in a different way than the streets ever made me. Clean tired. I'm proud tired.

I rolled home quick to shower and change, then pulled up to my spot to grab that pearl white G-Wagon I rented for Halloween night. Hit K's place just in time to see my little vampire prince running out the door.

*"Daddy!"* TJ squealed, the plastic fangs in his mouth almost falling out. *"This is the coolest car ever!"*

*"Only the best for my little king,"* I grinned, fixing his collar. *"We gonna hit up them big houses in Southern Trace tonight. They be giving out them full-size candy bars."*

I'd matched his vampire fit, everything black with a cape. *"Father-son vampires taking over the streets,"* I told him, loving how his eyes lit up at the matching costumes.

K looked like a whole dream, wide hips and fat ass on full display in her tastefully done Playboy Bunny costume. As she snapped pictures on her phone while I lifted TJ onto my shoulders. Her breast sat up high callin' my name. After a full day of learning new skills, bein' close to her and holding my son up high felt like the most natural thing in the world.

*"Look mama!"* TJ called out. *"I'm taller than everybody!"*

*"You sure are, baby,"* she laughed, and damn if that sound didn't make the whole day's fatigue disappear.

I had the whole route planned out, every house with their crazy decorations mapped like I used to map territory. But this was different. This was about making my son's night magical.

Between houses, TJ kept me laughing with his questions:

*"Daddy, you think real vampires are scared of anything?"*

*"Probably scared of brave little boys like you."*

*"Even with my fake fangs?"*

*"Especially with them fangs, son. You looking extra scary tonight!"*

When his bucket got too heavy, we hit up this fancy spot for dinner. Over chicken fingers and fries, TJ was already planning next year's costumes.

*"Maybe next year we can all match,"* he suggested. *"Like a whole vampire family!"*

*"Whole family,"* I repeated, catching K's eye across the table. The love there made everything, the long day learning new skills, the sore muscles from real work, the complete change in lifestyle, worth it.

Later, driving home with TJ passed out in the backseat, looking like a little vampire king surrounded by his candy kingdom, I reached for K's hand.

*"Thank you,"* I said softly, focused on the road.

*"For what?"*

*"For giving me a son worth changing for. For letting me be a part of this."* I squeezed her fingers gently. *"For the chance to make things right."*

Looking at my sleeping son in the rearview, thinking about my first honest day's work, holding the hand of the woman I never stopped loving, everything felt right. Tomorrow I'd be back in them steel-toes, learning more about building things that last. But tonight? Tonight was about building something even more important. Making memories with my family.

*"Happy Halloween, Trey,"* K whispered.

*"First of many,"* I promised. And for the first time in my life, I knew exactly how to keep that promise. By givin' her and my son, one honest work day at a time.

# CHAPTER TEN
# FORGIVENESS ON THE RISE

The moon was shining bright over the patio, throwing silver light across K's face while our son slept inside, probably dreaming 'bout his vampire adventures. Empty candy wrappers and Halloween decorations were scattered through the apartment telling the story of our perfect day, but right here? This moment between us was heavy with five years of words we both been holding back.

K sat close enough I could smell that coconut oil in her hair, rocking one of them oversized hoodies she always loved. Some things don't change like how she still had that habit of playing with her rings when she was nervous, still biting that bottom lip when she's thinking too deep.

*"You remember that last night?"* she finally asked, voice whisper soft. *"Before everything fell apart?"*

*"Every single detail."* I moved closer, drawn to her like a magnet always been there. *"You was wearing them scrubs with the little hearts. Hair up in that messy bun. Beautiful even after grinding for twelve hours straight."*

She smiled soft, but her eyes stayed sad. *"I had the pregnancy test in my pocket the whole time. I was gonna tell you that night, but then..."*

*"Then I came in running my mouth about the hustle, about making moves."* The memory seemed different now. *"Never even asked about your day. Too caught up in my own shit to see you was trying to tell me something that would've changed our whole world."*

*"When you said you ain't want kids..."* Her voice cracked a little. *"It felt like my whole world crashed. Here I was, carrying your baby, and you talking 'bout 'havin' kids ain't part of your plans and that shit ain't worth discussing.'"*

*"I was young and stupid, K."* I reached for her hand, relief flooding through me when she let me take it. *"So focused on being somebody in them streets, I ain't realize I was already everything to you."*

She turned to face me, and damn if that look in her eyes didn't take me straight back to them first days. *"You're different now. The way you move with TJ... it's like watching the man I always knew was hiding under all that street shit."*

*"Listen,"* I said, squeezing her hand delicately. *"I got something I need you to know. This ain't just about changing for TJ, though he the biggest blessing I ever got. This about being the man you deserve too."*

*"What you mean?"*

*"With me workin' a legit job now as a crew chief at Key Stone Construction with benefits, a 401K, and everything proper."* My thumb traced patterns on her palm. *"What you say 'bout you and me jumpin' the broom? Now that I'm legit. You don't have to worry about no more streets, no more looking over our shoulders. We can build something real now."*

*"For real?"* Her voice held that careful hope I was working to deserve.

*"For real. I want you and my son with me and for us to be a real family. A proper family with you being Mrs Taylor with all the benefits and rewards. What you say?"* I pulled her closer. *"I wanna do right by our family."*

Before she could respond, a small voice called from inside: *"Daddy? The monsters back..."*

We both stood up quick, parent instincts kicking in. Found our boy sitting up in bed, his big eyes wide with fear.

*"What kind of monsters we dealing with, little man?"* I sat on his bed, pulling him close.

*"The scary ones,"* he whispered, clutching his vampire cape like armor. *"They hide in the dark corners."*

*"Bet. Let's handle this."* I stood up, making a show of rolling up my sleeves. *"First thing you gotta know about monsters is they are scared of love. And ain't nobody got more love than us right here."*

K watched from the doorway while I did a whole monster checking routine by looking under the bed, in the closet, behind the curtains. But I made sure TJ was helping, teaching him the *"special moves"* to keep monsters away.

*"See this?"* I showed him how to make a heart with his hands. *"This right here stronger than any monster. Know why?"*

"Why, Daddy?"

"Cause it's filled with how much your mama and daddy love you. There ain't no monster bad enough that can stand up to that."

After we cleared every corner of his room and TJ was settling back down to sleep. "You know what else, son? Daddy got a new job now. Building houses and stuff. That mean I'm gonna be here every single night to keep them monsters away. You good with that?" I told him as I sat on the edge of his bed.

"Promise?" His whole face lit up.

"Cross my heart." I drew an X over my chest. "Your daddy done with everything except being your daddy and loving your mama right."

Once he was sleeping peaceful again, me and K ended up back on the patio. The moment felt different now, it was cleaner somehow, like them monsters we just chased away had been living between us too.

"You meant that?" she asked softly. "About being done with everything except us?"

"Every word." I pulled her into my arms, feeling right for the first time in five years. "Like I said, I got my legit job, got my son sleeping peaceful, got you looking at me like maybe we got a second chance. The streets can't compete with that."

"And are you sure you're ready this time, Treylon? Marriage is for keeps."

"I've never been more ready for anything in my life K. I want it all, K. I want my family back. I want to come home to you and TJ every night, help with homework, chase away monsters, build something real." My voice dropped low, just for her. "I'm still in love with you, baby. I never stopped."

When our lips finally met, it was like that first time all over again. Soft then deep, five years of missing each other pouring out in one kiss.

"Show me," she whispered against my lips. "Show me this real."

"However long it takes. Whatever you need." I held her face gently. "This our real legacy right here. Not no street fame, not no hustler's rep. Just us. Our family. Building something that's gone last forever. Say yes K. Say you'll marry me?" I pleaded.

She stared in my eyes like she was weighing my soul. "Yes Trey. I'll marry you," She nodded.

Standing there under that moon, holding my queen who agreed to be my wife while our son slept peaceful, knowing I had honest work waiting in the morning. I felt like everything finally made sense. Cause some hustles ain't

41

about paper or respect. Sometimes the biggest blessing is finding your way back to the love you almost lost and being man enough to hold onto it forever this time.

*"We got this,"* K whispered, fitting perfect against my chest like she never left.

*"Yeah, baby. We got this."* I kissed her forehead gently. *"One honest day at a time."*

# CHAPTER ELEVEN LOVE UNDERCOVER

I knew from jump that falling for Treylon wasn't in the plan, but once I got close, there was no stopping it. Being around him, learning his ways, I got in too deep. This whole assignment kicked off when Breanna Wilson put in a tip with the Shreveport Police, calling Treylon Taylor out by name. She painted him as one of the top dogs in Louisiana's biggest operation, which was all the DEA and FBI needed to step in. My role? Get close, get the intel, find his supplier. But it's been a year and a half, and in all this time, he's never let me in on his moves. I've never even seen his home. Every meet up was casual hotels, restaurants, clubs, and the latest nail salon disaster.

Falling hard wasn't part of the deal, but Treylon? He knows how to treat a woman right and got my mind twisted with the way he handles things. It's like heaven every time we're together. So, when I had to blow my cover three days ago, all because armed men came charging into the nail salon with high-powered weapons, I was mad as hell.

What really set it off was Breanna. Right before the raid, she'd dropped some info about Treylon having a kid with her cousin, loud enough for him to catch every word. That's when I figured out she's related to his ex. Later, when my supervisor and I questioned her, the truth came out. She's bitter as hell, upset Treylon never took her up on all those advances she threw his way, even after he'd broken things off with her cousin. Instead of moving on, she wanted payback and thought this investigation would hurt him. She even tried to ruin me, going straight to my supervisor, dropping our relationship into the mix.

*"Is that true, Constance? You've been with the suspect?"* David Winslow, my department head, asked, eyes fixed on me.

"Yes," I admitted, dropping my head and gritting my teeth to hold it together.

David's stare cut like a blade, then he turned to Breanna.

"*Ms. Wilson, I'm calling an officer to escort you out. Given your...revelations, this investigation is done,*" he said, voice sharp.

"*What? Why?*" Breanna screeched, almost losing it. "*I know he's selling drugs!*"

"*You ever seen him selling drugs? Do you know where he's selling drugs from?*" he fired back, his voice so hard it made me jump.

"*No, but he rolls with the dope boys, drives fancy cars, and has stacks of money. He's a drug dealer. I know it!*" Breanna screeched, sounding more unhinged by the second.

David and I shared a look, and I could see the exact moment he realized Breanna was on something else entirely. Frustration tightened his face. I'd been with Treylon for a year and a half, and despite digging everywhere, I hadn't seen a single sign of illegal activity. There were no shady deals, no drugs, not even a hint of it from his friends. That whole botched robbery at the nail salon only made things worse, exposing me for nothing. Now it turns out Breanna had us chasing Treylon for no more than petty jealousy. It's ridiculous.

"*Ms. Wilson, you do understand that filing a false report is a criminal offense, right?*" David snapped.

I kept my gaze down, feeling a strange sense of relief. At least now, the case would get dropped because of Breanna's nonsense, not because of my involvement with Treylon. A mark like that on my record would've been the end of this career for me. But now, we could walk away from this mess clean, knowing this whole investigation was a dummy mission from the start.

David pressed the button by the door, and a moment later, Chief Ottis Graver walked in. He scanned the room, folding his arms across his chest, then glanced at David.

"*What's going on here?*" Chief Graver asked, his voice firm.

"*Chief, this investigation is officially over. Turns out we shouldn't have started it at all. Ms. Wilson here initiated it based on...personal grievances. She's admitted to having motives that have nothing to do with criminal activity, and certainly not anything tied to drug dealing in Louisiana. In truth, she has personal connections to Mr. Taylor and used the system to pursue her own vendetta."* David straightened up and explained.

*"I'd say a nice, long stint for filing a false report and wasting taxpayer money is in order. What do you think?"* He glanced at Breanna, then back at Chief Graver awaiting his response.

*"Agreed."* Chief Graver nodded, giving a look through the glass. The door opened, and two officers stepped in.

Two officer's walked over to take Breanna to booking. When one reached for her arm she went ballistic.

*"Take your hands off of me. What are you doing. Let me go..."* she shouted until the door closed behind them.

The lights in the Shreveport Police Department interrogation room buzzed overhead, casting harsh shadows across David Winslow's face as he stared me down. The air reeked of stale coffee and cheap industrial cleaner, making my stomach turn, or maybe that was the anxiety eating at me, knowing my whole world was about to implode.

*"Let me get this straight,"* David said, his voice carrying that calm before the storm tone that made every agent's blood freeze up. *"You've been sleeping with Treylon Taylor for how long now?"*

I shifted in the metal chair, the cold seeping through my designer jeans, jeans that Treylon had bought me last month at that boutique in Bossier City. The memory made my chest tight.

*"About eight months,"* I admitted, the words tasting bitter on my tongue.

*"Eight months."* David's laugh was hollow. *"Eight months of compromising this entire operation because you couldn't keep it professional. And we had to find out from this..."* he gestured toward the two way mirror where Breanna Wilson had been sitting earlier, her mascara streaked face twisted with what I now recognized as more than just jealousy, there was something unhinged in her eyes.

*"I ain't mean for none of this to happen,"* I said, my professional facade cracking as my voice slipped into the Louisiana drawl I usually kept hidden. *"You don't know what it's been like, trying to get close to him, seeing who he really is..."*

*"Who he really is?"* David's fist came down hard on the metal table. *"Who he really is, Agent Bradley, is a suspect in what was supposed to be the biggest drug*

*trafficking case in Louisiana history. Except now we know there probably ain't even a case, because some jealous female with apparent borderline personality disorder decided to use the federal government as her personal revenge squad."*

The walls felt like they were closing in. My purse sat heavy on my lap, and I knew that pregnancy test was still in there, burning a hole through the designer leather. My period was two weeks late, and the morning sickness I'd been fighting lately wasn't just from guilt.

*"I get it,"* I said softly. *"I fucked up. But you don't gotta tank my whole career over this. We can close the case because of Breanna's false report-"*

*"No."* David's voice cut through the air destroying my hopes. *"We're closing it because you compromised yourself. That's going in the official report. You know why? Because if word gets out that the DEA and FBI got played by some scorned woman's false tip, we'll be the laughingstock of every federal agency in the country. Better to have one agent go down for misconduct than the whole organization look like a joke."*

From somewhere down the hall, Breanna's screams echoed off the concrete walls. *"He was supposed to want me! Not that stuck up bitch all over again! I saw him first! He was supposed to be mine! Why does Kiara always have to win?"*

I closed my eyes, remembering how Treylon had looked at me three days ago in that nail salon, when everything went to hell. The recognition in his eyes when I drew my weapon, the hurt that flashed across his face before it hardened into something I'd never seen before. The man who'd held me at night, who'd whispered sweet nothings in my ear and made love to me like I was his everything, he'd disappeared in that moment, replaced by a stranger who now knew I'd betrayed him.

*"Take some time off,"* David said, his voice softening just slightly. *"File your paperwork, clean out your desk. Maybe look into private security work. You know how this goes down from here."*

I stood up on shaky legs, my hand instinctively going to my still flat stomach. Treylon's baby might be growing inside me right now. A baby made from lies and undercover op gone wrong but made from love too. A real, messy, complicated love that wasn't supposed to happen. I wasn't supposed to fall for the Opps.

As I walked out of the station into the humid Louisiana night, I contemplated my next moves. *"Can I even make things right with Treylon if I am pregnant? Would he ever trust me after such a betrayal?"*

My heart stopped at those thoughts, then started again double time. Maybe some things that start with lies can end with truth. Maybe some loves are worth risking everything for.

But first, I had a date with a pregnancy test and a whole lot of soul-searching to do.

# CHAPTER TWELVE A NEW BEGINNING

The night air wrapped around us like silk, moon hanging fat and bright over Shreveport's quiet streets. Everything felt different now, cleaner somehow, like God himself done wiped the slate clean and said *"bet, try again."*

Kiara sat with me cuddled up on the lounge chair, both of us watching the Halloween decorations sway in the late-night breeze. My queen looking like everything I ever wanted and lost everything I was ready to cherish right this time.

She turned them doe eyes on me, the ones that always saw straight through my street facade to who I really was. *"I been doing a lot of thinking, Trey."*

My heart damn near stopped. *"Talk to me, baby."*

*"The past twenty-four hours been like something out of a dream."* Her voice was soft but sure. *"Watching you with TJ today... seeing how natural you two are together... it's everything I used to pray for."*

*"K, I swear on everything—"*

She pressed her fingers to my lips, gently.

*"Let me finish, Trey. Please."*

I nodded, kissing her fingertips before she pulled them away.

*"Five years ago, we was both young and scared. I ran 'cause I thought it was the only way to protect our baby. You was running too. Running from responsibility, from growing up, from being the man I always knew you could be."* She took a deep breath. *"But today? Today I saw that man. The one who dropped everything to be there for his son. The one who made our baby feel like the most important person in the world."*

*"He is the most important person in the world,"* I said, meaning every word. *"Him and you both."*

"I know that now." She reached for my hand, her soft fingers linking with mine like they was made to fit together. "So, I made a decision. I want you in our lives, Treylon. TJ needs his daddy. But..."

"But what?" I asked her, squeezing her hand. "Did you change your mind that quick? Decide not to marry me?"

"No. Of course not," she sighed. "I want to marry you and we be a family. I believe we can do it right this time."

"Then what's the problem?" I asked confused.

The smile she blessed me with coulda lit up the whole city.

"I don't want us to make the same mistakes. Last time we had a breakdown in communication. If I wouldn't have been scared and you would have listened. Maybe just maybe we wouldn't have lost five years together." She exhaled. "So, what I propose is that we talk things out. No matter how delicate, no matter how bad or good. We need to talk it out. No rushing, no pressure. Just... us communicating and finding our way back to each other. As a family."

"I can work with that." I pulled her closer, till her head rested natural on my shoulder. "Anything you need, K. Any pace you want. Long as I get to be here with my son... with you...us married and together."

"Us together forever." She looked up, moonlight catching the tears in her eyes.

"Always been you, Kiara. Even when I was too caught up in the game to show it right." I wiped her tears away tenderly. "You my endgame. You and TJ both."

The love in Kiara's face when she heard him... man, that's what real treasure look like.

"Who would've thought?" she whispered. "All these years running from each other, and Halloween brings us back together."

"Maybe it ain't Halloween." I pressed a soft kiss to her forehead. "Maybe it's just time. Time for me to be the father TJ deserves. Time for us to heal what broke. Time for me to love you right."

She snuggled closer, fitting perfect against my side like she never left.

"Promise me something, Trey?"

"Anything."

"Promise me this ain't just another hustle. That when things get hard, 'cause they will get hard. That you won't ghost on us again."

I turned to face her full on, needing her to see the truth in my eyes.

49

"K, listen to me good. *The streets, the game, all that old life? It's done. My new purpose is right here, being TJ's father, earning back your trust, building something real with our family.*" I touched her face softly. "*That's my word. That's my bond.*"

Her smile was brighter than any star above us. "*Then we got a deal, Mr. Taylor. I'll marry you and be your wife.*"

"*Bet that, Miss Kelly.*" I grinned, pulling her close again.

"*Mmm,*" she hummed, relaxing into my arms like coming home. "*You coming back was the best Halloween surprise ever.*"

Sitting there with my queen in my arms, our son sleeping peaceful inside, I knew without doubt that this was the biggest blessing of my life. Forget them streets, forget the hustle. My real empire was right here. And this time? This time I was gonna be the king my family deserved.

We started off with hesitant touches carefully building the mood. Neither one of us wanted to take the chance and break the fragile peace between us. Yet when her lips met mine, tentative at first, but it didn't take long for that spark to catch fire. My hands slid down, pulling her closer, our bodies fitting together like a lock and key. Five years was a long time to be apart, too long, and every touch, every kiss felt like trying to make up for lost time.

Her fingers tangled in my hair, pulling me deeper into her. "*I'm right here, Treylon. You got me.*"

I felt a surge of something smutty, real, that kind of need that went beyond desire, it was raw, naked, hunger, something that had been starved for too long. I pulled her closer, my hands roaming, my lips trailing along her neck, tasting the salt of her skin. She shivered, and that was all I needed to keep going, to lose myself in her.

"*Treylon,*" she whispered, her voice breaking, breathless. "*I don't wanna hold back no more. I want you. I want this.*"

"*I feel the same, baby. Ain't nobody else ever made me feel this way. Just you.*"

Her fingers gripped my shoulders as I shifted her back, removing her sweat pants. Then I quickly pulled down my black jeans and slid into her, "aahhh." She gasped. My body pressed hers on the lounge chair the wooden frame surrounding the patio our only cover under the stars. I pumped in vigorously. Her breaths comin' quick, matching mine, and I could feel the heat building between us, the weight of every stroke an unspoken vow, every moment we'd let slipped away we'd reclaim.

She looked up at me, her lips parted, eyes shining, and I could feel every piece of her, right there, as I slammed deep inside her velvety warmth. It felt like I was her entire world just like she was mine. And I didn't ever wanna leave that feeling.

Then, just as my lips brushed hers again, a shrill ringtone sliced through the night, cutting through the quiet, through the passion, like a splash of ice water.

We froze, my heart pounding, Kiara's eyes wide as we both stared at my phone, still vibrating on the patio table.

Both lost in the aftermath of unquenched passion. She looked at me, a question in her gaze. *"Who could that be?"* She asked.

I glanced at the screen, recognizing the name instantly, Constance Bradley. My gut twisted, and I knew I had to answer it. *"It's...it's that Fed. Constance Bradley. What the fuck could she possibly be callin' me for?"* I snapped. *"Let me get this real quick."*

*"Put that shit on speakerphone just in case she is on some fuck shit."* She reasoned.

*"Good idea."* I pushed the speakerphone button.

Kiara watched me as I placed the phone face up on the patio table, her brow furrowed. I leaned back and held her in my embrace, bracing myself, and answered the call.

*"Constance?"* I muttered, keeping my voice low.

*"Treylon,"* she said, her tone trembling, *"I didn't know who else to call. I'm... I'm pregnant. And it's yours."*

The words hit me like a punch to the gut. I felt the blood drain from my face, my whole world tipping on its axis. Constance. Pregnant. With my child.

Silence stretched, and I realized Kiara was watching, her expression shifting from curiosity to concern.

*"Treylon?"* Kiara's voice broke through my haze, grounding me. She looked at me with her doe shaped eyes, full of trust, full of love.

I couldn't lie, I couldn't even process this bullshit right now.

*"K..."* I began, struggling to find the words, but the weight of them settled like a stone between us, and I saw her expression shift, her trust shaken, her gaze searching mine.

# The End For Now...

# NOTE TO READER

Dear Reader,

Thank you so much for reading my book! I sincerely hope it provided you with a memorable experience.

As a new author in the fiction genre, I rely on feedback from readers like you to grow and improve. If you enjoyed the novel, would you consider leaving a review? It can be as short or as detailed as you like. You can post it where you purchased the book or on any other review platforms you use.

Your support means the world to me and helps other readers discover my work. Thank you again for your time and your thoughts!

I love to hear any feedback about my book and enjoy interacting with my readers, so please feel free to email me at rjackson318@allureproductionsllc.com authorrenessadjackson@gmail.com

If you would like to sign up for early notification of new releases, sign up here.

Thanks again!

Renessa D Jackson

# WHAT'S NEXT ON YOUR
# READING LIST?

I f you would like to read an unedited copy of the first chapter of the Chaos Wolf Series and the Savage Billionaire Series coming in 2025. Here is Chapter One of Chaos Wolf Ascending and A Savage Billionaire and His Ebony Queen.

# Chaos Wolf Ascending
# PROLOGUE Maverick Hollensworth

I paced back and forth in agitation in the center of the amphitheater surrounded by the gods who ruined my life. It was a giant monstrosity built like a Roman Colosseum with an open-air, oval shaped building with rows and rows of seats around a central area for outdoor gladiator games that seems to have been built exclusively to torture me. These bastards faked my death and broke the mating bond I had with my mate, all to bring me here to train to be able to train my daughter for some prophesized war to come in the future. They claim my sacrifice is supposed to save the world. In my opinion, fuck the world. I would have rather been there to see my daughter be born and been there to help my mate raise my son and my daughter to adulthood.

I can only imagine the hell my mate went through after losing me, then to have to go through a pregnancy alone, then birth. It's enough to drive an average person insane, and Gaia is an Alpha Wolf Guardian. The loss of a mate should have killed her, but the only exception is a pregnancy. Making her instinct to protect our pup override the need to join her mate in death. Just the thought of the pain she has been forced to endure because of my absence haunts me at night. That is on the rear occasion when I can actually sleep.

Apollo stood at the apex of the Colosseum with all the other Gods of Prophecy and War spread out around him. They all were looking at me as though I was causing them undo distress, but I don't give a fuck at this point. I have been trapped in this alternate reality for far too long. They all turned my life upside down, took my mate and children away from me and forced me into this Spartan training from the dark ages designed to shatter a person's soul in order to protect the world from the holy war they all keep harping about. It's been years since I've seen my mate and I'm passed fed the fuck up with this bullshit. Whatever else I need to learn I'll have to wing it because I'm though being their puppet.

"Apollo, why don't you let him go home now? There is nothing else we can teach him that he doesn't already know. He can best Mars, Tyr, Nyx, and Ares using both hand-to-hand combat and his various abilities. Let the man go be with his family." Morrigan spoke into the charged atmosphere.

She is the Goddess of battle and war, known as the Sovereignty Guardian Deity, who incites warriors to do battle and win gloriously even in death. Her bright orange-reddish hair sparkles in the sunlight making her pale freckled elfish face look otherworldly. Standing next to her you can feel the raw power vibrate off of her in waves. She was one of the few Gods that was against them handling things this way. Her, Phoebe, Tiresias, Brigit, Carmenta, Asclepius, and Thoth all thought I should have been allowed to stay with my mate and be trained in secret. They were all overruled by the majority, and that's why I'm here.

"Yes, Apollo. It's time. He has been here for 22 years and his daughter is an adult now. If he doesn't start teaching her how to control her abilities soon, this will all be a wasted effort. She has to learn how to control the power of Chaos are that power will consume and destroy her." Phoebe added.

Phoebe is the lunar goddess of the moon and her name means pure, bright, and prophet. Her grandchildren Apollo (Sun), and Artemis/Diana (Moon/Wolf Goddess), inherited their powers and names from her. She controls the Oracle at Delphi. She like Morrigan is a very beautiful goddess with diminutive features.

"Wait!" I shouted, "what do you mean it will consume and destroy her? None of you have ever said anything about her power being dangerous to her. You all said it was a divine power only gifted to the worthy and the blessed. Nothing about her being destroyed by that power speaks of a blessing," I snapped. "Explain." I roared getting all of their attention.

Brigit approached me wearing a sympathetic expression. "Calm down, Maverick. The Power Of Chaos can kill a God and destroy the world. Of course, it's a dangerous power. That's the reason we brought you here to learn how to control it. She has the power to save and/or destroy the world. Nothing about any of this is simple, and as you know, some of us would have handled you learning how to control it differently. That's all water under the bridge now. You need to focus on what happens next," she added softly.

"Well, let's get moving. I'm way pass ready to go." I grunted, ready to get the hell away from them all, and to see my mate and children.

"That's the problem. We can't come to an agreement on what would be the best way for you to reappear, that would be believable." Carmenta explained.

She is the Goddess of childbirth and prophecy. She is the protector of mothers and their children. She is the reason for midwives and she invented the alphabet to teach reading. She was also vehemently against me being separated from my mate and children. Since the first day I arrived she has been arguing about my return up till this day.

I frowned in confusion and shook my head, "what do you mean?" I asked.

"Do we return you as Maverick Hollensworth and fake a long term stay in a hospital in a coma, or do we give you a whole new identity so you can start fresh?" Thoth asked.

Thoth is the ancient Egyptian God of the Moon, judgment, wisdom, knowledge, science, art, magic, hieroglyphs, and writing. He is often shown in art as the man standing next to Sun God Ra with the head of a baboon or ibis. Just like in the depictions of him. He has hawk like features and a predatory presence.

"I would prefer to return as myself to be with my mate and children. Whatever we have to do to make that happen, let's do it," I sighed in frustration. "Have you all forgotten I need to train my daughter? Will she trust me if I appear out the blue to train her as someone else? Forget that. I want to be with my family. I'll go back as myself. Stick me in a hospital. How did y'all explain my death anyway?" I asked.

They all exchanged guilty looks. No one would look me in the eye. I got a sick feeling in the pit of my stomach. "What the fuck did y'all do?" I yelled.

They all looked over at me as my powers burst out of me slamming into them like a tidal wave. These Gods must have forgotten that they just spent 22 years training me to kill them, and I will, or die trying if they hurt my mate and children.

Ares, Artemis, Mars, Kratos, Indra, Odin, Nyx, Tyr, and Morrigan surrounded me. I was past rational thought at this point. They have been playing games with my family's lives for years. This shit ends today.

"Maverick please calm down and listen. It's bad, but none of what happened to your wife is our fault. Let us explain." Morrigan pleaded.

I instantly calmed down. Morrigan was one of the Goddesses I trusted the most. She helped me cope with the absence of my family by giving me a small glimpse of them from time to time. It was the only thing that's got me through this torture.

I took long deep breaths fighting to get my powers back under control. It took a great amount of effort since 75% of our gifts potential output can be significantly amplified by our emotions, and these fools showed me how combining them can change and elevate them exponentially. It took me over 5 minutes to reign in the destructive power rolling out of me. Once done, I sat on the ground breathing heavily.

"Explain." I demanded.

Morrigan sat down beside me with sadness in her vibrant green eyes. She reached over and placed a reassuring hand on my arm. "It's complicated, but I will explain what we know. After you disappeared and your mate bond was severed. Your mate was forced to breed with the other three Alphas in America to strengthen the bloodlines."

"What?" I looked at her in disbelief. They all gave me sympathetic glances with varying degrees of guilt. No one but Morrigan had the guts to look me in the eye.

"Yes. After you disappeared and the mate bond was severed. The American Wolf Council got together and forced Gaia to breed with the other American Alphas. They were hoping she would have a second chance mate with one of the other alphas. She has four daughters but is still unmated. Your mate has powers no other wolf has ever possessed and they all covet that power. She is the most powerful wolf on planet Earth, second only to your daughter. The best thing is no one knows about any of your daughter's gifts. She has been hiding them all except for her elemental powers that she got from both you and your mate." Tiresias explained. I looked over at him, not believing they kept all of this from me.

He is the blind prophet that transformed into a woman for years, known for his clairvoyance. He has the power to see the future.

"How could you all have kept this from me? My mate has suffered through some humiliating and horribly painful events over the past 22 years, and none of you saw fit to tell me about any of it until now," I roared. "Y'all can't be fuckin serious."

Apollo looked me in the eyes for the first time since all of this began. "Would you have been able to concentrate and learn all that you needed to learn knowing all of this was going on with your mate? No. You would have been distracted and you would have made us send you back without getting the knowledge you need to train your daughter. We did what was necessary to save this world." Apollo spewed.

"That wasn't your fucking choice to make, it was mine. My mate, my daughter, my son, our lives. You were wrong, and you know it," I spat. My power slipped from my control and Apollo flew across the ground and slammed into the far wall. His body made an indentation so deep five rows of seats were pushed back and destroyed.

Apollo pulled himself together blood coming from his eyes, nose, mouth, and ears. He walked back up to me slow and steady. You couldn't tell he'd just been magically bitch slapped.

"You done?" He asked.

I nodded, all the steam I had built up due to my anger evaporated. I just wanted to get home to my family. Everything else was irrelevant. I'm going home.

"I'm sorry these things happened. We all are, but we did what was required to save this world." He sighed and shook his head. "Let's get you home."

# A Savage Billionaire and His Ebony Queen

# CHAPTER ONE

Desiree stood in front of the floor length mirror situated in the corner of her room wondering where and when everything went wrong in her life. She was preparing for her 20th birthday party that was in fact nothing but a charade. Her parents were, in fact, trying to sell her off to the highest bidder, and it made her literally sick to her stomach. Just the thought that she meant nothing to them, but a high priced chess piece positioned on a board to provide them with the highest possible monetary and political gain was daunting.

They went all out planning the event to celebrate the occasion. No expense was spared and nothing but the best would be on display. Including her. What hurts the most is that the lavish event had nothing at all to do with her birthday. It was all about the so-called surprise engagement being staged. She was told to act excited when Rayvon Shaughnessy, the youngest son of State Representative Rashard Shaughnessy and Louisiana Circuit Court Judge Glenda Fisher-Shaughnessy proposed. This was a calculated move on her parents' part to link our family with the Shaughnessy family's wealth and prestige.

Our mother was known for selling her daughters to wealthy families to gain influence. It all started with the marriage of my sister Cassandra Strickland-Charles to her now husband Steven Charles 12 years ago. Steven is the heir to the prestigious Charles Investment Banking Firm. They are 3$^{rd}$ in line on the 10 most wealthy families in Louisiana list. Next is the marriage of our sister Rachel Strickland to Carl Grant when she was 22 years old, then William Maple at age 24, and Jack Kemp at age 28. Each of them cheated and the marriage ended in divorce.

Our sister Bridget Strickland-Miller married Chase Miller who is the heir to the Miller Textiles' Manufacturing Plant. They are the 6$^{th}$ richest family in Louisiana. Stephanie Strickland-Hampton, my fourth oldest sister, is married to Dewayne Hampton who is the heir to Hampton Pharmaceuticals. They are the 9$^{th}$ richest family in Louisiana and the deadliest. They are known to have connections to organized crime. Betty Strickland-Brooks, my fifth oldest sister is married to Jonathan Brooks airline pilot, and heir to Brooks Air-Charter Planes, and the 5$^{th}$ wealthiest family in Louisiana. Last is Jackie Strickland-Mims, who is married to Frank Mims Attorney, and heir to Mims and Sons Law Firm. They are the 4$^{th}$ wealthiest family in Louisiana and based in Baton Rouge, Louisiana.

Even with all that, I just thought things would be different for me because my parents have never once asked me to date or even entertain a man on their behalf before. So, you can imagine my surprise when my mother told me I was getting engaged to Rayvon Shaughnessy 3 days ago.

# Flashback 3 days prior:

I was sitting in my parents' den with my sisters discussing our sister Rachel's latest divorce and vacation to Paris. We all felt sorry for her because all of her husbands were dogs. Each of the arranged marriages that mother set her up with has ended in divorce due to her husband's cheating. Rachel has always been a rebel and would fight mom and dad to the end, but she always did whatever they asked despite her initial protest.

"I can't believe that nigga brought a woman into their home and slept with her in Rachel's bed. That was bold as hell," Stephanie snapped. "What kind of shit is that?"

"I agree. It's the lack of respect involved in that act that I can't understand. If he wanted out of the marriage, all he had to do was ask. Rachel didn't want his lame ass in the first place. So, she would have given him a divorce with no problems." Cassandra chimed in.

"It's ridiculous. She deserved so much more than that. Especially after all she did to help him build up his practice," Bridget added.

"Y'all all seem to forget that Rachel's problem is that she is an overachiever like the rest of us. She helped to elevate each of her husband's businesses and/ or statuses and then they all shitted on her because she outshined them in every way. Them nigga's egos couldn't take it. None of them nigga's deserved to be with our sister in the first place," Betty fussed. "With their jealous asses."

"That's so true," Jackie spoke up. "What's really sad is, if not for mom and dad Rachel would have married Giles straight out of college. She has been in love with that man since they first met back in high school. The only reason they are not together now is because mom and dad didn't approve of him back then. Now he's the top cardiologist in the country, and the highest paid one."

Desiree just listened to her sisters and nodded in agreement. We all knew that Rachel has been in love with Giles since forever, but she never went against our parents in matters like this. None of my sisters ever have. To be honest, I don't even think that Rachel divorced any of her husband's for cheating. It's the fact that they did it publicly that was the issue. Rachel told us that she has never been with any of her husband's sexually. So, they could fuck whoever they wanted to. They just had to keep the shit behind closed doors where it wouldn't embarrass her. Couldn't none of them stupid niggas even do that. Now that she's finally free from this last marriage. She went to get her man. I am the only one she told because she knew that I would keep her secret until after her divorce was final. She said she's done catering to mom and dad and their bullshit. It's time for her to live her own life for herself. That is if Giles is willing to forgive and forget. I believe he will because he loves Rachel just as much as she loves him.

I looked up to see mom walk in dressed to kill in a black and white Versace pants suit, black Givenchy heels, and her neck, wrist, and ears drenched in diamonds. Mom never did anything halfway. She always made sure she was the center of attention no matter what the occasion. Then with her killer body with dangerous curves to match her beautiful face she was every man's wet dream. At 52 years old mom was bad in every way and all seven of us inherited her beauty, brains, and business sense. Too bad she's a money and power-hungry monster that doesn't care who or what she has to sacrifice to get what she wants.

She stopped in front of me and paused for dramatic effect. Getting the attention of everyone at once.

"Now that I have your attention. I have an important announcement to make." She told us, grinning wide.

"What's going on Mom?" Cassy asked.

"As you all know. We will be celebrating Desiree's 20th birthday this Saturday at the Convention Center downtown," she cheesed. "Invite Only."

"Yeah. We know." Jackie chirped.

Mom gave her a glare and continued. "Well, what you don't know, is and I'm trying to tell you if you shut up. Is that it will also be Desiree's engagement announcement to Rayvon Shaughnessy." She smirked.

"What!" I shouted.

"Don't you dare take that tone with me young lady." Her mother snapped.

63

"I'm not trying to yell at you Mom, but I already told both you and dad that I can't stand that man. He makes my skin crawl with the way he undresses me with his eyes. That shit is creepy as hell." I screamed.

"Well, you can get over it. Your dad and I have worked hard to find you the perfect husband. He's rich, successful, and good looking. What more could you ask for?" She complained like my feelings didn't matter.

"I could want love, respect, companionship. I want to be with a man who sees me as more than a pretty face, and bad body. There is so much more to me than just my looks. That man is only interested in what's on the surface." I vented. Vexed at my parents lack of understanding in this situation. They act like I am purchasing a pair of shoes and not a life partner.

"Watch your tone, Desiree. I told your father that he spoiled you too much. Now you think you can do as you please, but you are dead wrong. We have already arranged this engagement and you will be there wearing a smile and looking happy when you accept his ring." She snapped and glared as she walked off.

My sisters all ran over and hugged me tight. I don't know how I was going to get out of this situation, but I refuse to marry a man I can't stand for my parent's benefit. Parents be damned.

The next day, as I sat in my room looking at the dress I was supposed to be wearing to the party. My mind drifted off to Carte. I met him when I first started high school my freshman year. I was only 14 years old at the time and he was everything I imagined my ideal man to be with his handsome muscular body. His good looks were not the only thing that made him so attractive. He was confident, dependable, supportive, hardworking, kind, committed, trustworthy, and most of all he got me on a level no one has ever before. He listened to my every word and made time to see me when I knew his time was limited. He worked every day after school and on the weekends so we were only able to spend a short amount of time together. Between him working and me hiding our relationship from my family, our time was confined to our lunch breaks at school and stolen moments on the weekend. Those brief periods of time we were together meant everything to me because I got to know exactly what it felt like to be loved and cherished by a man.

Since I was only 14 and Carte was 17 years old. There was a limit to what we could do as a couple, and due to that. I got to know him in a completely platonic way. I would watch him at practice for the basketball and football teams, and he would watch me at track practice. He would help me with my homework, so I was able to find out that he is incredibly smart. I even met and got to know his Aunt Connie who is his closest relative and most important person. Even now, she and I talk at least once or twice a week.

Carte has been gone for over 6 years without a word to me, and I still regret what happened when he came to see me after his graduation from high school. He stopped by our house, knocked on the door and asked to speak with me. I had no idea he'd been by until my mom came into my room and questioned me about what I was doing with that thug. I honestly didn't know what she was talking about because she didn't mention Carte's name and the person she described sounded nothing like him. That coupled with the fact that Carte had no idea where I lived made me believe it couldn't possibly have been him. Little did I know a week later I found out from the maid he'd been by when she showed me a picture of him that she'd discreetly taken with her phone. She told me how mom tried to embarrass him by telling him he wasn't good enough for me. I was so hurt because when I later saw him before he left and tried to apologize on my mother's behalf. He thought it was out of pity and not the genuine affection I have for him. I love that man and he is the only man I plan to be with.

Now I just have to find a way to get out of this stupid ass engagement. I will be going to the party and putting up with all the bells and whistles to keep up appearances, but I'm not marrying anyone other than Carte Blanche-Powell.

Coming out of her daydream. Desiree did a last minute check on her make-up and hair that was styled to perfection for this occasion by the top MUA and hairstylist in the city. Mom even went so far as to pick out my outfit. I can't complain since she chose a Vera Wang strapless black mini dress made of lace silk with black pearls throughout. It gave new meaning to the classic little black dress. She paired the dress with red bottom peep toe Christian Louboutin heels and the matching clutch tote. I kept the jewelry to a minimum with string chandelier diamond earrings with the matching necklace and bracelet. No rings. The total look came together well. Now I just have to keep the touching to a minimum.

---

DESIREE LET OUT A LONG breath and went to meet her parents in the foyer under the double staircase. Her mother scrutinized her appearance from head to toe. Her father tried to make small talk to relieve some of the tension in the air, but she had nothing to say to either of them. The drive to the convention center was strained, with the atmosphere in the limo oozing with toxicity and Desiree couldn't wait to get the hell away from both of them. After the 30 minute drive, the limo pulled up to the curb and the driver got out and opened the door for us to get. Desiree was the first one out of the door walking quickly down the red carpet. She didn't pause for photos with the photographers lined up outside to take pictures. She could feel her mother's dark glare on her back as she made her way to her sisters and their husbands standing off to the side of the entranceway. They were all wide eyed, not believing she left their parents and walked off not bothering to pose for a single picture, but they hadn't seen anything yet. Desiree refused to cooperate with this shit show. No one was selling her. She was not for sale.

As soon as she made it within touching distance Cassy grabbed her arm and pulled her to the side. "What are you doing Desiree?" She hissed. "Mom and dad are going to be pissed. I can see it in her eyes. She's mad as hell."

"She'll get over it, because I don't give a fuck. I'm not their property to sell off to the highest bidder. Fuck them!" She exclaimed.

Briddy pulled me away from Cassy. "Calm down Desiree. I know you're upset, but this is not the time nor place for this. Let's just get through the party and we can discuss your options later."

"Yeah, Desiree. We all know you are upset, but let's not make things worse by acting out. Let's get through tonight first. We can deal with the fallout later," Betty added and the rest of them nodded in agreement.

Desiree gave them all a stiff nod, took a deep breath, and put on a fake smile. They all watched and waited for their parents to take pictures for all the reporters and answered a few questions. When their parents walked up Desiree didn't miss the menacing glare her mother threw her way. She rolled her eyes at her mom, eliciting yet another stony look, but Desiree wasn't fazed. She couldn't believe her mother had the nerve to be upset after the shit she set in motion.

Her father walked over and patted her hand. "You okay baby girl?" He asked.

Desiree looked into his eyes wondering if he was really okay with her mother trying to marry her off to that pervert. She couldn't tell if he was concerned about her wellbeing or his public image. She just nodded her head and headed through the double doors following the rest of the family.

The hall was well decorated and all of the who's who were present tonight. The Mayors of Shreveport and of Bossier, Governor, State Representatives Shaughnessy and Caldwell, Senators Givens and Delaney, District Attorney Lorian, Judges Parks, Franklin and McMillen, lawyers, doctors, and other elite businessmen all came out with their families to help Desiree celebrate her birthday. Everyone was here to rub elbows and be seen with the top 15% of the elite class. There were tastefully designed banners with Happy Birthday Desiree hung in different sections of the banquet hall. It all looked nice, but Desiree took no pleasure in the event, knowing she was not the real reason for the celebration. It all left a bad taste in her mouth.

Mom and Dad switched to business mode and went off to mingle. Desiree hung out with her sisters and their husbands. Most of whom were conversing with their families and other business colleagues. That lasted until her feet started hurting in her heels and Jackie caught her limping and suggested they all take a break in the rest area on the second floor of the Convention Center containing the lounge sofas and chairs. We were all looking forward to getting off our feet in these heels, when we approached the cracked lounge door and heard a familiar voice coming from inside.

"That's my spot, right there daddy. Give it to me harder. Harder!" We all heard and exchanged a shocked glance, grinning.

"Keep your voice down. I'm not trying to get caught up in here with you." Desiree heard Rayvon Shaughnessy say as she and her sisters burst through the lounge door.

Rayvon had a half-naked woman bent over the back of the sofa sectional with the bottom half of her dress pulled up to her waist and the top half pushed down to her waist. Leaving both the top and bottom halves of her body completely exposed. From the angle from the door, we could all see Rayvon's condom covered dick gyrating in and out of her in rapid succession. He looked up and saw us standing there and didn't even break his stride to acknowledge our presence. If anything, it seemed like it made his dick get harder so he started to fuck her with complete abandonment.

Desiree shook her head at his audacity. "I wouldn't marry your sick ass if you were the last nigga on earth, and my life depended on it. I'd die first."

He had the nerve to bite down on his tongue and lick his lips, while giving Desiree a long lingering appraisal from head to toe. The shit was turning him on. Lust bloomed in his eyes and they slid to slits.

"Let's get out of here Desiree. Once we tell mom and dad about this, I'm sure they will call this bullshit marriage off." Cassy told me as we all headed back out the door.

"I wouldn't count on it. You will be mine Desiree. One way or another. You can bet on that." Rayvon chuckled, and fuck ole girl even harder before shouting, "close the door."

We all rushed back down the stairs and told dad what happened. He rushed up the stairs with mom following close behind him. Shortly afterwards State Representative Shaughnessy and his wife rushed up the stairs. My sisters and I made our way around the hall speaking to people we knew, trying to salvage what we could of the remainder of my birthday celebration. While greeting the guest, I saw Casey, Krystal, and Samantha grinning while watching the stairs. I made my way over to greet them and let them know we were going to head out. Before I even got the chance to speak, Casey said some shit that rubbed me the wrong way.

"Desiree, I noticed your parents and the Shaughnessy's haven't come back downstairs yet. Is there something going on?" She asked in a voice dripping with sarcasm.

"Why I don't know Casey. Maybe you can tell me what you think is going on, since you tend to think you know everything anyway." Desiree used reverse sarcasm.

"Don't be like that Desiree. We all saw you and your sisters rushing downstairs to talk to your parents. Then they rushed upstairs followed by the Shaughnessy's. Something important must have happened, and we're all a little curious." Casey clarified.

"Casey, you do know that curiosity killed the cat. Right? Are you trying to die?" Desiree asked, looking directly into her eyes.

"Desiree let's go. I don't know why you're even still entertaining this hoe. You know she's green with envy where you are concerned. She can't stand that you're better than she is at everything. You need to cut her jealous ass off. For good." Jackie groused.

"Jealous! What do I have to be jealous of? Desiree is no better than me, and what's up with the name calling? That's uncalled for." Casey snapped.

"Careful with that tone, chilly. You know you want to be Desiree so bad you can't stand it. Everything she gets, you just have to have one or something similar to it. Every nigga that's ever liked Desiree you have tried to get. Even with y'all fake ass friends you have to be the center of attention. The only thing that ruins that for you is that you can't compete with my sister and you always end up with cake on your face." Betty taunted.

Desiree shook her head, not in the mood to go back and forth with Casey today. "I'll talk to y'all later. We're leaving, but you all can stay and enjoy yourselves. The party's not nearly over yet. So, eat, drink, and enjoy," Desiree told them and followed her sisters out with their husbands.

"I can't stand them bitches. They all think they are more than everyone else because they were married into the wealthiest and most influential families." Casey vented once Desiree and her sisters were out of earshot.

"You know the shit you just said would have had more of an impact if you would have said it to their faces instead of behind their backs?" Krystal asked.

"Are you trying to be funny?" Casey hissed.

"No. I'm trying to be real. I ain't none of Samantha kissing your ass. My family is good and I don't need your crumbs. You talk a lot of shit when Desiree ain't around but be on mute when you are in her face. That shit is foul, and I ain't finna bite my tongue to cater to you." Krystal shot back.

"Y'all need to stop. But Casey Krystal is right. You already know how Desiree's sisters are about her, and you still are saying stuff to make them go off. You need to stop doing that shit. We are all friends so the backbiting needs to stop." Samantha added.

Casey didn't say anything more, just watching Desiree and her sisters as they made their way out of the Convention Center. "I still wonder what's going on." She thought.

# STAY CONNECTED

## @
## Join My Email List

Stay up to date with everything happening in Renessa D. Jackson's world-including new releases, upcoming releases, sales, updates, giveaways, events, and more.

Newsletter Link

authorrenessadjackson@gmail.com

# CONNECT ON SOCIAL

## X
https://x.com/
Allure_Pro_LLC?t=BmAST0NE7pOAgwoMk_v6KA&s=09

## Snapchat
https://www.snapchat.com/add/
allure_prollc?share_id=XZnXibghlIk&locale=en-US

## Instagram
https://www.instagram.com/allure_productions_llc/

## TikTok
https://www.tiktok.com/@allure_productions_llc?lang=en

## YouTube
https://www.youtube.com/@AllureProductionsPresentsRenes

## Website
https://allureproductionsllc.com/

## Renessa D. Jackson Ratchet City Readers Facebook Group
https://www.facebook.com/groups/2070696710014497

# ABOUT THE AUTHOR

Renessa D. Jackson, a native of Shreveport, LA, was born under the vibrant sign of Aries in April. Her temperament personifies the bright optimism and meticulous organization that her zodiac sign suggests. Her journey through life's challenges has molded her into a determined and confident leader, traits that shine through in every aspect of her personal and professional endeavors.

Renessa's love affair with reading began in her twenties, sparked by the captivating worlds of Manga and Manhwa. This initial spark soon grew into a blazing passion that includes fanfiction, romance, and urban fiction. Today, she finds joy in exploring a wide array of genres, immersing herself in the diverse and rich narratives that books provide.

Her deep appreciation for literature seamlessly translates into her own writing. As an author, Renessa is excited to welcome readers into the vivid and dynamic stories that have been brewing in her imagination. "Luvin a Young Ratchet City Boss," her debut novel, marks the beginning of the Ratchet City Boss series, promising many more enthralling tales to come.

Contributing to her bustling life, Renessa is surrounded by a loving family, including her six children, grandchildren and host of extended family members and friends.

Renessa continues to call Shreveport Louisiana home, where she is a cherished and active member of the literary community. She treasures the connections she makes with fellow authors and readers who share her passion for storytelling.

# ABOUT THE PUBLISHER

Allure Productions LLC is a dynamic publishing company dedicated to bringing powerful, authentic stories to life. Specializing in urban fiction and diverse narratives, we're passionate about amplifying unique voices and delivering captivating tales that resonate with readers. From raw street fiction to heartwarming romances, Allure Productions strives to publish stories that inspire, entertain, and connect with audiences on a personal level. With a commitment to quality and creativity, we're building a platform where compelling stories find their way into the hands of book lovers everywhere.

# ACKNOWLEDGEMENT

I would like to extend my heartfelt thanks to Carla Hill and my Ratchet City Readers and everyone else who took the time to read my book and provide honest feedback and constructive tips for improvement.

Special thanks to Jonessa Johnson for enduring my wild mood swings and the numerous changes to the cover.

I am immensely grateful to Dr. Dee Davis for assisting with all the technical details that I worried about completing on time.

Shut out to Jaylen Davis for helping me with advertising on the different social media platforms. He is a lifesaver because I am lost in the social media world.

Lastly, I would like to thank my cover model and graphic designer for their patience with my steadfast resolve to remain genuine in my presentation.